Kentucky Voices

Miss America Kissed Caleb

Billy C. Clark

Famous People I Have Known

Ed McClanahan

Buffalo Dance: The Journey of York

Frank X Walker

Books by Billy C. Clark

A Heap of Hills
A Long Row to Hoe
Song of the River
Trail of the Hunter's Horn
Mooneyed Hound
Goodbye Kate
Useless Dog
The Champion of Sourwood Mountain
Riverboy
Sourwood Tales
To Leave My Heart at Catlettsburg
By Way of the Forked Stick
Creeping from Winter

Miss America Kissed Caleb

Stories

Billy C. Clark

THE UNIVERSITY PRESS OF KENTUCKY

Published by The University Press of Kentucky

Scholarly publisher for the Commonwealth,
serving Bellarmine University, Berea College, Centre
College of Kentucky, Eastern Kentucky University,
The Filson Historical Society, Georgetown College,
Kentucky Historical Society, Kentucky State University,
Morehead State University, Murray State University,
Northern Kentucky University, Transylvania University,
University of Kentucky, University of Louisville,
and Western Kentucky University.
All rights reserved.

Editorial and Sales Offices: The University Press of Kentucky
663 South Limestone Street, Lexington, Kentucky 40508-4008

07 06 05 04 03   5 4 3 2 1

Library of Congress Cataloging-in-Publication Data

Clark, Billy C. (Billy Curtis)
  Miss America kissed Caleb / Billy C. Clark.
    p. cm. — (Kentucky voices)
  ISBN 0-8131-2296-1 (Hardcover : alk. paper)
  1. Kentucky—Social life and customs—Fiction. 2. Appalachian Region,
Southern—Fiction. 3. Mountain life—Fiction. I. Title. II. Series.
  PS3505.L2425M575 2003
  813'.54—dc21   2003011400

This book is printed on acid-free recycled paper meeting
the requirements of the American National Standard
for Permanence in Paper for Printed Library Materials.

∞ ❀

Manufactured in the United States of America.

 Member of the Association of
American University Presses

Contents

To my wife, Ruth; my son, Billy; my daughter, Melissa; and my three grandchildren, Benjamin, Timothy, and Jodie. To Earl and Jeanie Lockwood. And to Tina Dean. These stories for your keep.

Miss America Kissed Caleb

It was July 1942 and my older brother, Caleb, and I had been on the mountain since daylight picking blackberries that Ma wanted for cobblers, jams, and jellies. We had picked her a bucket before high noon and another gallon of our own to sell off in Sourwood for a dime, which would buy us two nickel ice-cream cones. Then we would drop off at the edge of town to swim in the Sourwood River, cheating the heat and washing away the chiggers we had gathered picking berries on the mountain.

That was our plan, at least. It had been a hard morning, one that I thought would never end. Dodging briars to reach the berries, we fought temptation to eat the soft dewberrries instead of dropping them into the buckets, which would have left us with blue tongues and brought a fierce scolding from Ma. She believed that while in the patch berries belonged inside a bucket instead of the stomach.

The sun had been hotter than I could ever remember. The timekeeper in mountain country, the sun seemed to be caught in a blue background and unable to move. Caleb, often watching me suck blood from a briar-pricked finger, egged it on, grinning, shaking his head at the sun and singing, "The briarier the berry patch, the sweeter grows the berry." The sweet coldness of the ice-cream cone and the coolness of the waters of Sourwood seemed so far away.

Finally the sun, bumped by white clouds, had inched its way until it was directly overhead. With our buckets full, we headed off the hot mountain knowing that our trip into Sourwood was shorter with every step. With a mountain as its backside, Sourwood began with a narrow dirt road that ran along its edge and disappeared into the trees. Beyond this road, the trip led up a hogback just broad enough to hold two steel rails for a train, down the other side and across a narrow strip of level land that was Sourwood proper, and over the edge of that into the river.

Dry as seasoned wood and briar-pricked, we were climbing the hogback to cross the rails when Caleb stopped me with his hand. He was shielding his eyes from the glare of the sun and looking toward the small depot where trains stopped to take on water from the big wooden tower that had been built there for that purpose. Squinting, I saw a gathering of people looking off up the rails. The rails sparkled in the sun like two silver ribbons, growing closer together with distance until they disappeared as one farther up the valley. I heard the low sound of music drifting and knew that the Sourwood Mountain Boys were there, which meant a special occasion of sorts. Made up of local men, they played for funerals, revivals, baptizings, square dances, political rallies, and the sort.

Itching from curiosity and chiggers, I looked toward Caleb. Before I could ask him what he thought was up, he said he remembered that a troop train was due to stop at the Sourwood station in the early afternoon to pick up some local boys who had joined the army to make the war shorter. That being the case, Caleb reckoned, the least we could do was to help send them off proper-like, throwing in that it could amount to a one-way ticket, which left me hung between waiting for the ice-cream cone or seeming a traitor. To do less was to favor the other side.

"It won't take long," Caleb coaxed.

And so we made our way up the tracks and joined the crowd. A crowd that looked to include everyone from Sourwood and abouts. Most of the women were dressed in calicoes with figured patterns of every sort and sunbonnets with as many colors as autumn leaves. Most of the men wore bibbed overalls bleached out by time and lye soap.

Some of the older men had gathered to hold an ambeer-spitting contest using marks on the hot rails as targets. I could see the ambeer fly through the air and sizzle into nothing as it hit the hot steel. Closeness to the mark was told by knee slapping or hee-haws.

Women were busy gossiping, which they always do whenever there is more than one. While they talked, they fought to keep the kids away from the hot tracks. I watched one small boy break away and, barefooted, manage to stick his toe on the hot steel. He squawked like a wildcat and got a whipping to boot while his mother dragged him away. His crying brought crying from others his size and the noise was terrible. I sided with the boy; I knew that the burn had hurt. I was barefooted myself and even the earth beneath my feet was almost hot enough to burn.

Restless, thirsty, and itching terrible, I was about to ask Caleb if we could slip away when a yell went up from the crowd and the band struck up an off-key rendition of "Dixie." I watched as the big steam engine pulling the troop cars jerked down the rails, belching smoke, steam, and fire like a storybook dragon. Her brakes made a mournful sound as she pulled into the depot and squared up at the water tower. Steam and smoke covered us all like a cloud. It was hard to recognize anyone. But as the engine quenched her thirst at the water tower, the steam thinned enough for me to see some boys on the train stepping off to stretch their legs, stare around, and wallow in greetings from the people of Sourwood. Biding time while local boys said their goodbyes.

And it was then that she floated out of the steam and smoke, a young woman pretty as a night moth. Her dress was made from an American flag, and she wore a golden crown on her head with little flags, now wilted from the steam, sticking from the points of the stars up there. Her shoes were long and striped and looked like they had been carved out of two great blocks of peppermint. She waved a flag with one hand and held a bucket in the other. A short, winter-thin man moved in front of her, separating the crowd and saying, "Make way, make way. Make way for Miss America and give generously to help her bring our boys home!"

I heard the sound of coins ring the bottom of the bucket and her bird-sweet voice saying, "Bless you; bless our dear boys!"

"Where did she come from?" someone asked.

"Off the train," the answer came. "She's riding the long rails with our boys to keep them safe and mother-kept."

"Some mother!" an old man wrinkled as a hedge apple said, reaching out to touch her and getting his hand slapped by his woman.

"Gathering a little money for their needs along the way," someone said. "God bless Miss America!"

As she floated among those in the crowd, the ringing of the coins increased. The thin man followed closely, coaxing for coins, trying to keep the hands of the men off Miss America but permitting a child held high to touch her now and then.

"Give generously. Please help Miss America bring our dear boys home. She's making the long haul!"

Well, this set most of the women crying, and that scared the kids, and they cried too. Their mothers held them high so they could get a look, or a touch if they were lucky, at Miss America.

"It's Miss America," they wailed. "She's come all the way to Sourwood to help our dear boys."

"I've heard of her," another said, "but never thought I'd live to see the day she'd be in Sourwood. Must be the Lord's work, an angel sent to be a comfort riding the rails."

As she edged nearer to the band, they played louder. Maybe having run out of songs sad enough to fit the occasion, they struck up a hoedown that seemed on the verge of tempering the sadness. But Miss America took care of that. She waved her flag and it muted every string on every instrument except Joe Faraway's banjo, which he struck one more time as he dropped his picking hand. This brought mean stares from most everyone.

With the hissing of the big engine furnishing the background, she began to sing "God Bless America." Most of the men held solemn looks while the women still cried and the babies still squawked. It was all as sad as being around a corpse laid out. And, for shame, I took the time to remember an ice-cream cone, but regretted it some.

Money rang the bucket like a bell, and the people farther back in the crowd tossed their coins over the heads of others to land in the dust near her peppermint shoes. I watched the dust rise in little puffs as the coins fell, particularly a bull nickel that had landed on its edge and was rolling toward me. Figuring that all eyes were on Miss America, I waited until it was close enough and captured it under my big toe. I stared around independent-like to make sure no one in the crowd saw. But just when I thought I had caught in a second what it had taken a half bucket of berries to make, I felt my toe being lifted. I squinted down as the thin man plucked the nickel out from under my toe like the feather from a chicken. His look singled me out as a traitor, and I swallowed and looked to see if the crowd caught that.

Miss America glided closer now to where Caleb and I stood, leaning some, I thought, from the weight of the coins inside the bucket. She stopped directly in front of Caleb. I caught a movement from him out of the corner of my eye and saw that he was fumbling inside his pocket. Afraid of what I was thinking, I whispered, "What's up?"

"Maybe something what's right in my life for once," he answered. "Different from laying out of school, chewing tobacco, and the sorts."

The next thing I knew she was leaning toward Caleb, and he pulled *our* dime from his pocket and was holding it over the bucket, pinched between his thumb and forefinger. Knowing that I could be lynched by the crowd if I said anything, all I could hope for to save our dime was the way Caleb always was: tight as the bark on a log! She waited, but Caleb would not let go. I swallowed and then made the mistake of looking into the eyes of Miss America: sad, pretty, and able to coax a biscuit from a hound. If Caleb makes the same mistake and crosses her eyes, I thought, the way he is with girls, it's all over!

He did and didn't. I mean he crossed eyes with her but still held onto our ice-cream cones. I felt proud of him. He pinched the dime so tight that his thumb and forefinger turned white. I felt relieved that his want was as great as mine. She'd have to have something more than a stare to strip us of all the money we had in this world.

She did! She bent over and kissed Caleb on the cheek, and I watched our dime land on top of the other coins in the bucket. I heard the conductor hollering, "Board, board!" I heard the big engine hissing and watched Miss America disappear inside the steam.

After the smoke and steam had cleared, Caleb and I stood alone at the depot. The others had made their way toward home or into Sourwood proper. I stepped between the tracks to stare the way our money had gone. I caught a movement off the tracks where a short section of the dirt road could be seen. And there she was, Miss America with the thin man, making their way into the trees on the side of the road. They hadn't been on the train at all, I thought, but had drifted in from the other side of the tracks into the steam and smoke and out in a crowd that wanted them to be. Probably on their way now to another depot and another troop train that would surely come! Excited to think that we might overtake them and get our dime back, I nudged Caleb.

"Hurry!" I said. "They went that way!"

But looking at him I knew that he hadn't seen them; worse, I knew it probably wouldn't have mattered anyway. He was holding his cheek with his hand and staring off with eyes that saw nothing.

"Miss America kissed me!" he whispered.

And that was that. We never even went swimming.

The Ring

Caleb said that when it came to Thanie Miller you could be sure of three things for sure: that she had to be the ugliest woman ever born on Sourwood Mountain; that she was a witch-in-the-making because her ma, Pearl, was a witch and these powers were always handed down and ran in families; and that Thanie had never been with a man and was never apt to be, because of her looks and because Pearl never allowed her to be off out of sight.

On the first, I thought that Caleb was right, mostly. Especially in the beginning before I got a chance to know her close up. On the second, I wasn't so sure but was afraid to doubt. For to doubt something this powerful and then find out in the end you were wrong was too scary to talk about. Though Ma said witch talk belonged to boys Caleb's age who used it to go around scaring boys my age; that they went around searching for some poor widow woman who had troubles enough and then tacked her with being a witch, spreading tales to try to prove it. Why it always had to be a woman, she never knew, unless it was handed down on the man-side of the family along with other bad habits. But on the third, Caleb was dead wrong. For I had seen Thanie along the creek at

9

night with a man and kept that to myself. If I told Caleb, he was sure to tell the other boys he loafed with, and they would stake Thanie and her man out, and I would miss whatever took place between them. A close second for keeping it a secret was that if Caleb did tell and then Pearl found out that I had been a part of it and kept it from her and she really was a witch, I could be snuffed off the mountain. For Pearl had always guarded Thanie like a hawk, seldom if ever letting her out of sight. Especially as Thanie had grown and gotten more "naturals" about her to watch out for—though Caleb was afraid to tell me what "naturals" were because he was afraid I would go tell Ma whenever I got mad, or let it slip out. Either way, his life wouldn't be worth living after. And while Ma's reasoning why Pearl watched Thanie so closely differed from Caleb's, Caleb's was more exciting and made believing easier, especially out of Ma's sight or hearing.

And then, too, most times Caleb was all I had to whip the loneliness of the mountains, and I didn't want to have him mad at me. Caleb claimed to have "worldly ways" attached to him, especially when it came to girls. I thought he might be able to help me find out what to watch for down at the creek where I had staked Thanie and her man out. Add to that, Caleb told me if I was ever to mention to Ma that he had mentioned "worldly ways" to me, I could strike him off as a brother. I was left curious but cautious. I did ask him about "worldly ways," why he couldn't tell me.

"Ma, mostly," he said.

"How's that?" I asked.

"Simple," he said. "If Ma had her way she'd ruther we both stay tadpoles. She lost out on me, but she's still got you. It ain't for me to lead you astray."

Curious, I asked, "How come?"

"More than I can take a chance on telling," Caleb said. "But for one thing, a frog is 'worldly.' Old enough to know that they's girl frogs out there who he aims to find. Now a tadpole, he just lays off on the bottom of the creek bed thinking the world ain't nothing but sand and current. Slow growing up."

Caleb was smart. And often we talked long into the nights whenever we were sure Ma was asleep and wouldn't hear. We talked about Pearl and Thanie. Pearl being a witch and Thanie's ugliness. Sometimes he'd lean on an elbow and squint to be sure that Ma wasn't close, and he'd say things like, "Ugly, all right. Thanie is. She ain't the sort you'd stake out to see if and when she's washing off down at the creek."

Talk like that caused me to squint, too. Not really knowing why but sure that Ma would skin us out for talk of it. Caleb probably—hopefully—catching the worst of it because of his grownupitish talk that led me astray.

Ma did not take lightly to any gossip when it came to either Pearl or Thanie, and in particular Thanie. Over the years Ma formed an attachment to Thanie, even though she did not see her that often anymore. As hard as Pearl's life had turned out, it was Thanie that had had the worst of it, never having the chance to grow up knowing a childhood like she ought to have had. A child being forced into womanhood before her time and quicker than her mind could catch up, Ma said.

Ma told how Pearl had taken sick shortly after her man, John, had been killed deep inside a coal mine over on Blaine. So far back inside that they had never been able to recover his body or the seven others who had died along with him that day. The mine became his grave.

He had been a good man, a good provider with an eye for land and living. Just a year before he died he had bought a tract of land up Difficult Creek less than a mile from where our house sat. He pushed back the woods and built his cabin so it backed up to a sizable cave with enough room to winter-store cabbage, apples, potatoes, and the sort. Enough room inside to sink locust post to cradle wood and shelter it from the weather. He built two small stalls there out of dry sassafras boards he had bought down at the mill and made a place for a little yellow Jersey cow and a grey mare work mule no larger than a bank mule.

That winter he spent most of his time outside the mine clearing off a large strip of rich bottomland along the creek for a garden and never lived long enough to see the makings of a crop.

Pearl had never gotten over his dying. Buried where she could never lay beside him. The first Decoration Day after, she carried flowers to lay at the mouth of the mine, with Thanie trailing along behind her. When Pearl went back home, she took sickly and went to her bed. Talk was she had had a stroke. From that day on she seldom walked farther than the end of the yard. Wasn't able to. The burden fell on Thanie.

For a while after, women came visiting from a church in Sourwood; for spiritual reasons and to talk about Thanie's schooling since she had been taken from school after the death of her pa. Pearl had not taken lightly to that. Finally they quit coming.

Caleb said rumor was that Pearl got afraid that they might coax Thanie away, that she might run off with them. So afraid that Thanie might leave her, she welcomed no one coming, with us being the exception.

If Ma had ever visited much, Caleb and I never knew it. Since either of us had been big enough, she had sent us to check on them from time to time. Especially if Thanie did not come down creek and stop off on trips she made into Sourwood to buy supplies. Things that could not be raised on the land or found on the mountain. And now that Caleb was laying off mostly with other boys, going to check on Pearl and Thanie fell mostly to me.

Ma spoke often of Thanie. The burden she had. A neverend. Every day the same as the day before. Early of the mornings she helped Pearl out to the porch to a rocking chair where she sat the day, weather fitting. Thanie had to be close enough to come when Pearl called to move her either to the warmth of the sun or to find shade when she became too hot. Carrying water from the creek to heat and bathe Pearl off before the sun went down and the chill of the wind came down the mountain. And always with Pearl quarreling at Thanie's slowness and uncaring ways. Caleb said that if you ever got nerve enough to be on the mountain above her house you could hear her quarreling like a jaybird.

Caleb said that even Thanie's trips into Sourwood were had-to-be and timed. That Pearl, having made trips there herself before she had gotten next to bedfast, knew exactly how long it took to go there, buy what was needed, and even stop to see Ma on the way back. She showed Thanie the hands on a clock so that Thanie would know.

Caleb also said that what Pearl had come to fear most were man-things. Knowing the "natural things" that came to a woman. And when I asked him about "natural things," he told me that if he ever got tired of living he might tell me. But he didn't figure that time would be coming anytime soon. That in the meantime to keep thinking traps and gigging for suckerfish.

Too curious to quit pestering, I coaxed matter-of-fact-like, "Thanie's too ugly for natural things anyway."

"Look," Caleb said. "This is all I'm going to say about it: Naturals ain't got nothing to do with pretty and ugly. It's got to do with wants! You'll find out for yourself one day when your tail drops off and you sprout legs and get the urge to leave the sand. Which is a ways off. Then, too, having naturals ain't all a bed of roses. It ain't like a creek to seine and suckers to gig and listening to the birds sing. Naturals are worrisome."

"What do you mean by that?" I asked, feeling a little uneasy.

"I mean you get eyeing Thanie the wrong way on one of your trips up there to Pearl's and your world could change overnight if you're still around to see it. She can throw a curse to the top of a mountain! You'll find out about fooling with naturals."

"Ain't no reason for Pearl to see anything in my eyes," I said, and then to get on Caleb's good side, "Thanie's too ugly for me."

"It ain't what she *ought* to see," Caleb said. "Never is with a witch. She sees what she *wants* to see. I'd be careful if I was you!"

Thanie being the way she was, I couldn't see how Pearl could make anything of it as far as I was concerned. You saw Pearl, you saw Thanie, mostly. Thanie favored Pearl more every time I saw her. She was thin, short, man-like in ways. Especially when it came to her nose, which Caleb said she took after her pa, though I wondered how he would know something like that being that he had never seen her pa. Her fingers were long and always red from washing clothes with homemade soap. She wasn't still long enough to look at if you had wanted to. Washing or hanging clothes on the line for the wind to whip dry or splitting wood two sizes. One size for the cookstove, the other to fit the grate for an open fire. Carrying water up from the creek was her longest trip, with Pearl timing her even there, nervous, rising up and dropping back in the chair and yelling for her. Caleb said it never occurred to her that, turned loose, Thanie had nowhere to go, if even she wanted to. The life she had was all she knew, had ever known.

Thanie's face had leathered from sun and wind, and sometimes her hands so cracked that Ma gave her herb salve to heal them. Like everything else that was small enough to hide, Thanie stuck the salve in her bosom. To hide, Caleb figured, from Pearl. Ma never said anything, although she knew that she was doing it. Pearl did not allow Thanie to wear lipstick or rouge or use perfume. Nothing, Caleb said, to pretty-up. And so she smelled of sweat most times. She kept her hair in a bun on the back of her head like an old woman. Her hair had started to grey at an early age, like Pearl, whose hair was snow white.

Thanie seemed scared of Pearl, and I didn't blame her for that. I was afraid of Pearl, too. Caleb made it worse telling tales of Pearl casting spells on boys that he knew and even loafed with. He told the one about Mick Daulton who had been given the evil eye over as little a thing as not wanting to turn loose of a boar squirrel.

Mick had strayed too close to Pearl's on a squirrel hunt on the mountain, and she had seen and forked him down with a finger. Knowing that a witch could throw an omen to the top of a mountain and he was only halfway up, he walked down. Up to the porch where she sat in a rocking chair. It was scary. Mick said the goiter on her neck was as large as a small pumpkin and had crooked her head so that she looked at him slanchwise. Her thin hair had fallen to one side like an old bird's nest shook loose by a strong wind. Saying that she had a taste for a mess of squirrel, she asked him to set a price on one. With thoughts of taking the long way home to do a little bragging on the size of the two squirrels he had caught, he hesitated. Casting around, he saw Thanie on the other end of the porch threading leather britches, and afraid Pearl might think she saw something in either his or Thanie's eyes that wasn't supposed to be, he glanced away.

"Well," said Pearl. "Be your squirrels to do with what you want. But my money spends. You could be sorry later on."

He should have taken that as a warning but didn't. Halfway home he saw another fox squirrel crossing over and cut down on it. The next thing he knew he was left holding the stock of his gun. The barrel had split down like shredded cabbage. Ruined.

Tom Preston was the next one to have a spell cast on him. His over as little a thing as a bucket of berries. Pearl had thrown a curse on his right foot that would cause him to limp for the rest of his natural life, not to mention the pain that went with it, especially when it rained. His story was hard to doubt; every time I saw him, he limped off something awful.

But Ma cast a spell on both stories when she overheard Caleb telling them. Ma said that Mick had told the truth about the barrel of the shotgun blowing up; the how of it was where he went wrong. Truth was, Mick had reached the ridge and lazied up, then leaned on the gun for rest with the barrel down, which put dirt into the end of it. And this wasn't the first time he had done that. The first time he had not blown the barrel off but put a bulge in it until it looked like a black snake that had swallowed an egg halfway down. He got a licking from his pa both times and should have.

As for Tom Preston, it seemed funny to Ma that whatever

Pearl was supposed to have cast on him caused him to limp only when someone like me was looking. Asked to check it out myself, I did, and truth be, Tom never limped when he thought I wasn't looking.

Still, both Pearl and Thanie had too much mystery and scare about them for me to gamble on, and so I decided to cut a swath around both except under threat of a have-to from Ma. And truth be, I might have stuck to it if greed had not set in.

I had gone into Sourwood to check on the price of traps at Ben May's store when I ran into Thanie, who was there buying necessaries. She had filled two sacks and told me that if I helped her get them home she would give me a bull nickel. To boot, she would show me a fresh mink track she had spotted on her way down the creek. Both were too much to pass up.

She helped me lift the lighter of the two sacks to my shoulder, with me asking for the heavier one. She refused, and as tiny as she was, she shouldered it like a man.

When we reached the mouth of the creek she started right off talking varmints and trapping and the big mink track she spotted below her house, in the bend of the creek under the sycamore that stretched its roots out into the creek like a spider. She knew the mink had gone up the creek and could be gone for some time since minks liked to travel, being the curious varmints that they were. A mink would travel by land or water, and here on Difficult Creek he would cast off to check out every cave or deserted mine along the way looking for field rats and the sort. She had even found mink tracks in the cave behind her house, mainly, she figured, because they kept no dog on the place. She knew too that one day the mink would come back down the creek and follow the path he had used to go up. A trap set without people-scent, and in the right place, would take him.

She told me that she often saw weasel tracks in the cave. And lost a chicken to them now and then although she set traps to catch them, traps that had belonged to her pa. She knew it took a

smaller trap to take weasel because their bones were frail and a trap
too powerful would cut through the skin and bone and you would
lose him. She told me she would search and see how many double
aughts were at the house.

She talked of how the muskrats had stolen corn from the
corn patch below her house, and how they tunneled under the high
banks everywhere along the creek. The entrances to their holes
were underwater and then curved up inside the bank to dry land.
She showed me where they had pulled stalks of corn into the creek
and stripped off the blades to pull into their homes for bedding.
Some of the blades still stuck out of their holes, quivering in the
current like water snakes. She wondered why I had not bothered
to set traps there before. I was ashamed to tell her I was afraid her
ma might see me there and cast a spell on me. She coaxed me to
come to trap, and I made a promise that I would, not knowing that
I would really keep my word. She told me it would please Pearl,
and I did think that pleasing Pearl might be good for me, too.
When she told me that Pearl liked muskrat fried-up now and then,
I even promised to bring one.

She talked of herbs and how to make willow chairs, the frames
by soaking willow limbs in the creek until they were soft enough to
tie like strings, and the seats from hickory bark stripped off tall
saplings and also soaked in creek water. She would even teach me
how to make a chair and give it to Ma for a Christmas present.
Told me that Ma was her best friend, her only friend that she
claimed.

Time and distance went by so fast that we passed my house
before I knew it. Thanie talked like she had stored up words forever and was just now letting some go. She stopped to show me
some tall tulip poplars that grew along the creek because they liked
for their roots to be in moist earth. She asked if I knew how much
honey a wild bee could find in a single blossom when the trees
were in bloom. For shame, I couldn't, so she told me there was a
spoonful of nectar in every blossom. She asked if I knew what

color the honey was that came from poplars. I was more ashamed than ever, and she told me it was dark honey, called "sarvis honey" here in the hills.

She told me that the soft earth along the rock ledges that lined areas of the creek was where wild leeks grew. And that the earth they grew in was put there by rain and wind. That above the rocks under the locust groves the wild shawnee grew, the best of the wild green. That it could be cooked alone or used in a mix without taking over.

I asked how she had learned so much about the mountain and the creek. Her answer was simple. Her ma liked soft crawdads, frogs, turtles, and things of the creek, and she used to go there to get them. Even sometimes in the backwater catching large carp and buffaloes and canning them for winter. She had learned the ways of the mountain from Pearl. Add to that what had been self-taught. But now Pearl hardly left the yard and needed her close.

I was so tied up in what Thanie said that when we walked into the yard I forgot that I would have to face Pearl, that I was about to be the closest to her I had ever been. Maybe the closest I would ever be, if I was snuffed out.

Pearl was sitting on the porch watching the path she knew Thanie would be coming on. When she saw us she waved a feeble hand and even smiled. Which for a moment took some of my fear away. But then I remembered that more flies were caught with honey than vinegar and I got scared all over. She looked so old and scary. Wrinkled as a hedge apple, she was winter-thin and pale and her mouth sunk in from no teeth. Her head rested on her right shoulder, bent there by the goiter on her neck, which caused her to have to look sideways. Just as I was thinking how witchy she looked, using mostly what Caleb had told me to go on, she spoke. A low feeble voice with a touch of quiver to it.

"Favor your ma a lot, you do," she said. "Natural though. You can tell a Hewlett. Strong people. They mark their children." She kept staring at me. And then she smiled. "Why don't you put the sack down and get shed of your burden. Good of you to help Thanie home. Could be I'll reward you."

I swallowed, not sure that this wasn't how the end would be. She made it worse by turning her head slow as a turtle and then quarreling at Thanie.

"What took you so long?" And then just as quickly as she said it, a smile crossed her face and she said, "End of the month is always a busy time. Payday at the mines, you know. Lordy, it gets lonesome here without John."

She crooked her finger, motioning for Thanie to come closer, and Thanie moved quick as a cat. When she whispered something in Thanie's ear I turned hoping Pearl would know that I wasn't about to listen to what she was intending to hide from me. I saw Thanie smile and it helped some, unless Thanie had witch-ways too. And then Thanie went into the house and left us alone. But not for long. She came back and handed Pearl something that I couldn't see and hoped she saw I wasn't trying to.

Pearl forked me to come closer, and I think my heart stopped. The only thing left was for my past to start coming up before me like it would whenever your time had come to leave this earth. And although Caleb had said it would take awhile for mine, the way I'd been and what I'd have to answer for, I didn't figure I had much time left. "Here," I thought I heard her say. I opened my eyes wider. I stuck out my hand, and she dropped a bull nickel in it. And then, seeing the surprise on my face, she said, "Come back tomorrow and help Thanie gather a little corn and winter wood, and there could be more where that come from."

From greed and fear I promised, not knowing which was the stronger of the two. I turned to go, but she stopped me in my tracks.

"Wait," she said. Figuring my luck had run out, I stood there mortified.

"Stay long enough to help Thanie move me to the other end of the porch and catch the last of a dying sun. The air has turned chilly. It's hard on Thanie, me being crippled like I am."

Moving her was slow, awkward, and hard. As we worked to move her I wondered how Thanie was ever able to do it alone. We started with Thanie backing up to Pearl like a mule to a singletree. When she felt her legs touch Pearl's she stopped and bent backwards, telling me to put my hands under Pearl's armpits and to lift her high enough to wrap her arms around Thanie's neck. I swallowed, closed my eyes, and did what I wouldn't have done for all the bull nickels on the mountain if I'd had a choice. To make matters worse, when I lifted her the goiter brushed against the side of my face scaring me like a ghost. For some strange reason I wondered if a goiter could be catching like poison ivy or oak. Or, if she could cast it on me.

Once she had straddled Thanie's back, Thanie shuffled slowly toward the other end of the porch, turtle-slow, telling me to follow and make ready with the chair. When we got there, Thanie backed up to the chair and dropped Pearl like a sack of feed.

At the edge of the yard I stopped and glanced back and saw that Thanie had brought a pan of water from inside the house. The steam rose from it, and I figured Thanie was ready to bathe her down. From the smell of her armpits, I figured she needed it. I wouldn't have told her that. But I planned to wash my hands at the creek using sand for soap.

I was glad to be going home before dark. The rocks and heavings of the earth along the path became the goiter on Pearl's neck, and the sough of the wind her wheezing voice. I saw her ugly face over and over again, and I thought of what she had said about the Hewletts marking their children and how much Thanie looked like her. Except for the goiter and a handful of other things, with their backs facing, it would have been hard to tell the difference. And yet Thanie was not that old at all.

When I reached home Caleb was there, and once away from Ma's seeing or hearing he fussed. Mainly because I had told Ma about the bull nickel. Both Ma and Caleb were displeased, but for different reasons. Ma thought I should not have taken the money but waited for my reward from Higher Up. Telling me that good things happened for them that gave of themselves without taking earthly rewards. I should have done it for nothing and watched for signs of good things to come. Caleb was against my taking the money because I wouldn't loan him some, knowing that I saved it for winter trapping. He also told me to watch for signs, but not the kind Ma was meaning. Signs that the money was tainted and carried a curse on it. Time would tell. I had probably brought a curse home on all of us. Carried it like cockleburs. He was one thing; but snuffing out my own Ma for a bull nickel was something else!

Caleb fussed even more when I told him I had landed a job up there. "You best keep your eye on that old woman," he said. "I could tell you more about her spell casting, but you'd probably tell Ma I told you!" he studied. "You get too close to Thanie and your goose is cooked. Truth ain't got nothing to do with it. Pearl's mind has gone bad!"

But in the days that followed I even got to where I was looking forward to going. When it came to the creek or mountain, I judged Thanie to be the smartest person I had ever known, outside of Ma. She worked like a man, as little as she was. Good with a crosscut saw, she taught me how to let the saw do the work. Showed me how to size up a block of hickory and almost stare it into splitting. How to wedge knots. That cedar and pine would blow out a fireplace but were the best for kindling. We dropped hickory saplings and skinned the bark from them and then rolled the strips into round bundles to soak in the creek. Learning was a never-end.

Each day Pearl seemed less witchy. I was leaning toward what Ma said about Caleb being bad to pack tales about old women. But not quite. I kept my eye on her when I was sure she couldn't see me. Truth was, I was afraid of the old woman, and more so the times she quarreled at Thanie for little or nothing. Thanie was hardly more than a slave. But then, at times she treated Thanie like she was still a child, as if she was trying to make up for it. It was then that I thought of Caleb saying that rumor was her mind was going away.

And then one afternoon when I had gone inside the cave in back of the house to help stack wood, Thanie walked behind the wood and motioned for me to come around where she was. She seemed nervous, squinting toward the house as if she was afraid Pearl might come out the door, even knowing full well that Pearl was not able to raise herself from the chair and walk alone.

I had no idea why Thanie wanted me back there. It made me nervous too. I squinted toward the house myself. And when I looked back around I couldn't see Thanie, and for the moment that scared me. I whispered her name, not knowing why I was whispering, and heard her answer softly, "Come back here."

I swallowed, squinted toward the mouth of the cave one more time, and walked around behind the stack of wood. Thanie was on her knees, and stretched out before her was a dollhouse she had made with blocks of wood. She had whittled wood that formed a table and chairs. At one end was a small bed with tiny blankets and all. Her knees had pushed the soft earth in considerable, and I could see that she had been here often and over a long period of time.

"I come here to make the loneliness of the mountain go away," she said. And then reaching down inside a hole she had dug out in the floor of the cave and had covered with a board, she pulled out two dolls and held them to her chest. She saw me staring at them.

"They're store-bought," she said. "Saved my money and bought them a long while back at Ben May's General Store with the promise of a no-tell. Some from skimping on things like yard goods Ma let me buy to make my clothing and some from the sale of berries and herbs I gathered along the creek and traded without Ma knowing."

And then acting as if she was trying to see through the holes in the cord of wood if Pearl was coming, she added, "Know how I got them past Ma?"

Not being able to imagine, as close as I had come to know

Pearl watched her, I whispered, "No," and wondered why we were both whispering.

"Guess," she said.

I thought for a moment. And then remembering what Caleb had said and I had come to know, that whatever she wanted to hide past Pearl she put down her bosom, I said, "In your bosom?" nervous about how she might take my knowing.

She grinned and fooled me. "No, silly," she said. "I brought them here when I didn't have anything up here to show," and she patted her breast. "Ma would have caught that right off. I brought them here inside my bloomers."

If she saw the redness of my face she never let on. She was holding the dolls now. One had long brown hair and the other short dark hair. She pushed the short-haired doll toward me.

"Look," she said, "a man doll!"

She quickly pushed the two dolls close enough to one another to kiss. And then, seeing the blush on my face, she said, giggling, "Don't worry, silly. Look."

She pointed out the ring that she had fashioned on the finger of the girl doll.

"It's a ring," she said. "They're married!"

And then as if I was not there, she started playing house with them, talking to them as if they were real people. With little else that I could do, I went around to the other side and started stacking wood. She raised up once and looked over the stack.

"You won't tell Ma on me will you? If she was to find out, especially about the man doll, she'd whip me good!"

"I won't tell," I answered, making a promise that I knew somehow I would have to keep. Told, what might happen to the both of us was too scary to think.

"Promise?" she asked.

"Promise," I said.

And I left her there playing with the dolls, passing up Pearl and the bull nickel this time. Leaving Thanie to get Pearl inside on her own. I walked home carrying the biggest secret I had been asked to keep. And wishing that I had never known.

I worried about it until I was afraid of being sick. I worried about giving the secret away without intending to. A word here or there that Caleb could build on. He could piece a rumor out of little or nothing. Maybe I would talk in my sleep!

One thing was certain: if Caleb found out it would spread over the mountain like a flash flood. I could only imagine what it would be built into. Especially when it reached Sam Puckett. Sam had the longest tongue on the mountain, and not even Caleb stood a chance of out-topping him. Got it from his Aunt Dixie, who had died a year ago over on Nebo and passed it down to Sam. A tongue so long that when Dixie died they had to keep her up three days longer than usual waiting for her tongue to stop! That Ma said Dixie had been a gospel woman carried little weight; a story like Caleb's was too good to pass up.

Not the least of my worries, though, was Pearl. She had changed so much in the short time I had come to know her close-up. She had grown weaker and more forgetful, sometimes to the point of forgetting to pay me. But who would have told her that! At times she mistook me for Thanie and quarreled at me like I was her own child. Accusing me of not caring about her and the sort. Of trying to sneak off and leave her to die alone.

My only reprieve was that with winter not far off I had to help get in our own winter wood and spent less time at Pearl's. But whenever I was away for several days, Pearl would forget who I was and try to run me off, thinking I had come to sneak Thanie away. Thanie would make over her and say pretty words to her. It was almost too sad to bear. If I had not come to know Pearl and seen the ugliness and change creep up a little at a time, she would have been too scary to look at.

And yet, as hard as my secret was to keep, it ended up a nothing compared to what was to come: a secret that was only mine to keep and as big as the mountain itself.

It happened one evening when I was coming home after dark. I had chosen to come by way of the creek so that I could pick up the level land and have better footing. Then, too, it gave me a chance to check on Pearl and Thanie even though I would not be stopping. I would be able to see the light from the oil lamp that always sat on the table and imagine Thanie inside rubbing Pearl down because of the old woman's arthritis.

Just this side of their house, I heard a voice along the creek up ahead of me. I listened, and hearing it a second time, I knew it was Thanie's. She often came to the creek either to get a breath of air and relief from Pearl or to fetch a bucket of water to use for washings and the sort, their drinking water coming from a shallow well dug close to the house. I thought Thanie might be talking to herself, which she often did. I did, too, for that matter, the mountain being a lonely place and all.

But when I got closer I heard another voice. And this one belonged to a man! Curious, I sneaked closer and took up watch within sight and hearing behind a clump of elderberry bushes. A safe place, I thought, where I wasn't apt to be seen unless someone knew I was there and was searching.

The man was a stranger to me. But that was not unusual. Sourwood was a river town and caught its share of drifters off of boats that plied the rivers. Few, if any, stayed long, rumor was. Caleb said the lucky ones pushed on downriver. The next luckiest ones got run off in one piece. The less lucky floated away or ended up in an unmarked grave chalked up to whiskey or the wrong poker hand.

Thanie was holding a bucket to fetch water, or to fool Pearl that water was what she had gone for. They were standing behind a grove of willows out of sight of the house. He was holding Thanie's hand, pulling her closer to him.

Then I heard Pearl's weak voice calling for her from the house. I knew that Pearl would be sitting in the doorway squinting into the darkness trying to make out the path that led to the creek. She never allowed the door to be closed while Thanie was out.

"I can't stay," Thanie whispered.

"Wait," he said, pulling her close enough to kiss her. She made no effort to pull away, and he kissed her again.

Pearl hollered again, and Thanie pulled free, breathing so hard that I could hear her.

"Coming, Ma," she hollered back.

"Tomorrow night, then?" he whispered.

"I'll try," she said.

She stood staring at him for a moment longer and then disappeared up the path to the house. I watched him standing there staring, rubbing his hands on his britches before turning down creek and off the path onto the mountain.

Sure that both were gone and not apt to come back, I headed home with more burden than I thought I could carry. My head was full of what I had seen and heard. Things I had never thought I would ever hear or see. There were moments that I was even mad at Thanie for what she had done. And without knowing why; like she had tricked me same as she had Pearl. That it was not her right to be on the creek with a man. A man I didn't know but disliked. One I pegged a drifter—the worst sort, because Caleb said so. He had drifted away from somebody once before and would hurt and leave again. Even Ma had little good to say about drifters, because they never held steady work and always had a casting eye and a fiddler's foot.

I remembered Caleb saying that Thanie was too ugly to catch a man. I wondered what he would say if he knew she had kissed one! I thought of the dollhouse, the two people she kept inside, together only because the girl doll had been given a ring to make things right. The only reason she could hold the dolls close enough to kiss.

And then, too, for shame I thought about the kiss. What it might have been like. I worried about Pearl finding out somehow, maybe through witch-ways and all, and knowing that I saw and heard and kept it from her. It was all too scary and sad to ponder on.

When morning came, I tried to busy myself searching for signs of varmints along the creek. But when dark came I took up my place behind the elderberry bush and waited. I heard him coming up creek long before I saw him. Even Thanie said I had the ears of a squirrel. He waited. I waited. But this night Thanie never came. After a long wait, he left. And, glory be, I felt cheated. Cheated out of seeing what I had faulted Thanie for doing.

The next night she came. And then the night after. In the days that followed they met often, and I was always there. Growing more curious and cautious, I came back of the days to clear away any signs I might have left behind the bush the night before. I became afraid that Thanie might come along the creek for whatever reason and spot a sign that I had been there. Like Ma said, whenever you were doing something you were afraid of getting caught at, even the mountain appeared to have eyes. Add to that, Thanie knew signs, which gave me even more reason to worry. I worried about odors, remembering how she said a mink could sniff you out without seeing you, knowing you were there without your leaving tracks. To fool him, you boiled traps in walnut hulls to take the odor of steel away, and you traveled by water with sacks tied to your shoes to make a set for him. I had used nothing.

The way things had changed now, at night was about the only time I got to see Thanie. Truth be, I missed her. And in some ways, I missed the old woman, too. Pearl had become so pitiful. As far as I could tell, Thanie had changed her mind about getting me to help her gather corn or add more firewood inside the cave. And once when I saw her along the creek during the day and asked her about circling some tree to die standing and cut later for firewood, she told me the sap was still up and that if we cut before the sap went down it took forever for the log to season and burn right.

But she never forgot to slip down to the creek on nights to meet up with the drifter. And I never forgot to be there, for that matter. Their meetings had become longer and more exciting. They sat now on soft leaves pulled from the willows, keeping them off the damp ground. Done so, I figured, knowing poor Pearl could not walk down to see or hear. They kissed and whispered so low that I feared getting caught straining to hear and see. She whispered things like "stop" and "a kiss is enough." And one night I watched him pinch her breast. She jumped up. I never knew whether she would have sat back down or not, for Pearl hollered and pleaded.

He got up but pinched her again, kissing her again and again. She pulled away.

"It ain't right!" she said.

"Maybe it ain't ever going to be right," he answered angry-like. "I mean, we got no reason to sneak around like we do. We ain't doing nothing wrong. Nothing that ain't natural!"

And for the spare of a moment, I wondered if this was the "naturals" that Caleb had spoke of.

"It would kill Ma if she knew," Thanie said.

"I ain't kissing the old woman!" he answered. "But I'm beginning to wonder who's killing who! Don't you want a life of your own?"

Thanie started crying, softly. "Ma needs me," she whispered. "I'm all she's got. She would die without me."

"Then you might die with her," he said. "You ain't no prize looker with time to choose!"

And when she cried louder, he apologized for that and kissed her softly.

She answered Pearl back.

Then, before she left, he pulled her to him again and kissed her. She had to slip from his arms, struggling to pull away. As she did so, he pinched her breast again.

"It ain't right," she said again, but she never pulled his hand away.

"Then let's make it right," he said, letting go. "See you to-morrow night?"

"I'll try," she answered, with her voice saying she would.

The next morning on my way up creek passing her land, she

fooled me by waiting on the creek for me to come. At first I was afraid she might have found signs that I had been there the night before. But then I saw a corn knife in her hands. She handed me the knife and asked if I was free to cut some corn to shock. She would be able to help me on and off, but since Pearl was having a bad day, she would have to leave me alone now and then. When I got tired I was to stop and then bring back some ears to the house with the corn knife.

Working the corn, she said very little. Nothing like she had always talked when we were together before. She stopped once to show me the waste of rats in the corn and said that Pearl would be even madder about that. Especially their taking out a few rows of corn to carry to the creek. When her pa was alive he had told her ma that rows of corn were like the strings of a dulcimer the wind played to make pretty music. Taking out corn was like breaking the strings, stealing the music. She and Pearl often sat on the porch to listen to the wind in the corn, just like Pearl and her pa had once done. I had heard wind in corn before too. It was a sad song. With Pearl's hearing gone bad, she couldn't hear the wind in the corn anymore.

I left Thanie that evening pretending to be going home but didn't, afraid something might come up and that I wouldn't have time to get back to watch what happened between her and her man. I even worried that he might not show up or that Pearl might take worse and Thanie wouldn't be able to come down to the creek. I breathed easier, but quieter, when they both finally showed.

They kissed right off and sat down on new leaves that made no crinkle. They laughed about how old leaves made noises. But as bad as Pearl's hearing was, I thought, they were free to cheat on her all they wanted. As for me, I could see and hear it all!

Thanie lay back to stare at the sky, and he quickly climbed on top of her. She jerked and slid out from under him, swatting at her dress where she had rolled off the leaves and onto the soft dirt.

"It ain't right!" she said, dusting her dress off and standing up.

Pulling himself up, he grinned. He reached into his pocket.

"I figured you'd say that," he said. "Well, let's make it right!"

He opened a small box, and I saw him hand her something. When the light from the moon crossed it I saw that it was a ring. Thanie started crying. She glanced off toward the house and then started to drop the ring inside her bosom. He grabbed her hand.

"It don't go there," he said. "It goes on your finger. And once on, it don't come off."

She started to put it on her finger but stopped. She stared toward the house again and then along the creek, and I thought for a moment she might have seen or heard me. I was straining and breathing too hard.

"Put it on," he coaxed, "or, let me."

She pushed his hand away but kept the ring balled up in her fist.

"It would kill Ma," she said.

"Or us!" he said, louder than I thought he ought even if Pearl could hardly hear. "Put it on!"

Not answering, Thanie just stood trembling like she was caught between a want and a can't.

"It's your chance to break away," he said. "A chance for the two of us. Put the ring on."

"But what will happen to Ma?" she said.

"How could I know or care?" he answered back. "I ain't marrying the old woman. You going to put the ring on or not?"

Thanie said nothing. He shuffled his feet, and I knew he was angry.

"You ain't no child, you know," he said. "How much more of your life are you planning to waste? It ain't that you got choices, you know!"

And then seeing that what he said made her cry harder he tried to kiss her, but she backed off.

"Then give me the ring!" he said.

But Thanie only held it tighter. He reached out and twisted the ring out of her hand.

"I ain't taking on some damned old woman to keep!" he said. Holding the ring for her to see, he said, "Choose!"

Thanie never moved.

And then he threw the ring into the brush along the mountain and stomped off.

For a moment I thought Thanie was going to go after him. But after a few steps she stopped. I heard Pearl begging. And then Thanie picked up her bucket without water in it and turned toward the house, crying.

I wondered what would happen when Pearl saw that she had been crying. But then I thought surely Thanie had been caught crying before and had found a way out. She could do it again.

For a few days after, I returned to the creek each night waiting to see if they came again. Thanie did. She sat on old leaves and watched and waited, fidgeting at the least movement or sound as if she expected her man to walk out of the trees and join her. I did, too. But he never did, and Thanie gave up coming before I did. Finally I gave up and turned to other things.

Thanie had become more distant now. I saw her sometimes along the mountain below the house scratching around in the leaves where the ring had been thrown. If she saw me, she told me she was looking for an herb. But I knew what she was looking for. And doubted that she would ever find it. Harder than finding a needle in a haystack. Even a crow could have carried it off.

At times I saw her in the field gathering corn for feed. Once she told me she was turning the yellow Jersey dry so she could build strength to have her calf. I thought of the fun it had been the times Thanie spent teaching me to milk her. How at first the Jersey had refused to put her milk down for me because she didn't know me. And Thanie telling me she could do that, although I believed at the time Thanie had already milked her out and was fooling me. Later, when the Jersey came to know me, she put her milk down every time. Pearl had not been as sickly then as she was now, and she had cackled and thought it was so funny. She said that it was the way of a woman to change her mind if she wanted to. That if I talked pretty she might come around. Thanie taught me to make butter and buttermilk and gave me some of both to take to Ma. She showed me how to make a pretty mold to shape the butter.

I wanted to help Thanie find the ring but couldn't without giving away that I knew what had happened. I knew that she would no more share her secret with me than I would share my secret with her. Thanie's search for the ring reminded me of a story she once told me about a ring that her pa had bought her ma, a wedding ring with a big stone in it. One day when her ma had gone to feed the chickens, in throwing out the feed she noticed that the stone was out of the ring. Figuring it had come off in the chicken lot and that a chicken had pecked it up for grit, her pa killed all the chickens and searched their craws. But the jewel had not been found. A week later she found the diamond out where she always threw the wash water. She told how they had foundered on chicken and that even now Pearl would not eat it.

Lonesome and curious, I thought of ways to visit Thanie without pestering. But it was Ma who gave me a reason. I had spent the day wooding the fire for Ma to make apple butter, and she asked me to take some to Pearl to go with morning biscuits. It would give me a chance to check on the two of them without seeming nosy. Ma was concerned because it had been a while since she had seen Thanie pass on the way to Sourwood.

I found them both on the porch, Pearl dozing and Thanie staring off toward the mountain. Pearl looked old and worn-out, her jaws sunken and the goiter looking bigger and more ugly than before. Her hair was stringy and drooped over her face so thin that it hardly shaded her eyes. In a screechy voice she told me to thank Ma for the apple butter and that she would have Thanie fix biscuits come morning. Thanie acted more distant. She took the apple butter into the house and came back with a comb. She started combing out Pearl's hair. Pearl quarreled that the comb was catching and hurting her head, and Thanie looked at me like Pearl was just wanting to have something to quarrel about but meant no harm. I knew that Thanie had long grown used to Pearl quarreling and paid little or no attention to her. She combed, saying, "Hold still, Ma! Hold still!"

Pearl answered, "You wouldn't think a child would talk back to her ma like that!"

Truth was, I missed being with Thanie. I tried to think of ways for coming again.

"Be needing to cut more wood?" I asked. And remembering what Thanie had taught me about weather signs, I added, "Black as the hair is on the wooly worms and how heavy the shucks are on the corn, I'd say it ought to be a hard winter."

Thanie grinned and added, "Or counting foggy mornings."

Thanie stared off toward the mountain. Fall had come to the land now, and already leaves were falling from the trees, many of them set to fly by wind that told of a change of weather. The land about was more visible now and the grey rocks stuck to the sides of the steep slopes, staring back like eyes sparked by a meager sun.

As we stared Pearl pulled her shawl more tightly around her and fussed at Thanie to be sure to keep the fire wooded and to have enough dry wood stacked on the porch to feed the stove so she wouldn't have to go out in the weather for it. She cautioned Thanie to be sure to keep the rest of the winter wood covered and to make sure there was enough dry red cedar split for kindling.

Of all the wood we worked with, I enjoyed splitting the cedar kindling the most. Everything about it kept me closer to Thanie. First, going along the slopes to find a cedar that had died standing. For these, Thanie had taught me, were the red ones, heartwood that was so red and shallow-barked that you could scratch the bark and expose the heart with a thumbnail. I had asked Thanie why a cedar that died standing was always red, different from the white cedars that were more plentiful but of less use. A red cedar would stand as a fence post for eighty years, a white one less years than it paid to put it in the ground.

As to why the cedars that died standing were always red she was not certain, although she was sure it was always true. Red was the heart of the tree, and she had heard Pearl say once that all things dying struggled to live and so built a bigger heart to survive. That they had lost in the end was easy to tell since the outer bark turned corpse-white and stood out on the land like old bones.

Thanie pleased me by asking if I could come during the following week to help her split and cord some shagbark hickory. We had blocked it out earlier in the summer, when Thanie had taught me to work the other end of a crosscut saw. But the following week splitting the wood did not turn out to be all that I had looked forward to. Even though the wind was keen, spitting flakes of early snow now and then, Pearl insisted on being brought to the porch to sit. She fussed over the cold and at Thanie for it coming to the mountain and for bringing her out in it. She accused Thanie of knowing she stood to catch cold and not caring. Thanie spent as much time going to the porch and wrapping the shawl around Pearl as she did splitting and cording wood.

Thanie passed it off by telling me that with trapping season close, I should be sure to make the set for the big mink under the giant sycamore she had pointed out back in the summer. To hide human scent, she told me to stay in the water while making a mink set and to always cover the trap with leaves from the bottom of the creek, leaves water-soaked and sure to stay over the spoon and the jaw of the trap and not give way to the current. I wondered how Thanie could have learned so much, become so mountain-smart having to watch Pearl all the time.

Near the end of the week things got worse with Pearl. Thanie said she was having a bad time of it and so passed off her quarreling and fussing. Worse, she took to forgetting who I was, judging me to be someone who might try to coax Thanie off. I would have to go to the porch and let her stare and feel around over me. Her head now drooped, exposing the big goiter more than ever.

Once back splitting wood she fussed that the noise was too much to tolerate and that we were doing it only to aggravate her.

Nearer the end of the week she did not recognize me at all. Thanie told me I had best go since Pearl didn't want anyone around now except her. She would watch for me coming up creek to make trap sets and would wave if she was in the yard and saw me.

I tried to busy myself now with trapping, but the mountain was lonely and miserable. I thought the season would never open. But it did and I set out to make my first set for the big mink under the sycamore. I took great pains in making the set, trying to fool myself that I was simply following the ways that Thanie had taught me but knowing that slowness gave more time for her to appear in the yard and wave at me. She never did.

The wind carried winter with it now, and it was cold along the creek. At times the snow was spitting so heavy I could barely make out the frame of the cabin.

I had trapped the better part of the winter when I came home just ahead of a circuit rider who stopped in the yard to tell Ma that Pearl had passed away. He had been preaching on Nebo Mountain and turned down Difficult Creek to stop for a word of prayer at Pearl's. Opening the door because no one answered his knock, he found her dead in a chair inside the house. He found Thanie sitting in a chair beside her, asleep. When he woke Thanie, she called for Pearl and tried to wake her. He judged Pearl had been dead for at least two days; she had gone to smelling.

Taking a glass of water, he said that no way could he make Thanie believe Pearl had died, and that she refused to leave her and come with him because she feared Pearl might wake and need her, or holler, not hear, and go to quarreling. He told Ma that he was on his way to Sourwood to fix up a burial and that he would be back with someone to dig the grave. Ma promised that she would go to Pearl's immediately to care for Thanie. She told me that I was not to go with her. I was too young to be exposed to a corpse.

Ma left, and before she returned I saw two men pass the house with picks and shovels. I knew they were going to bury Pearl.

Her grave ended up being just above the cabin. Thanie said she wanted Pearl close so she could watch over her. Ma let me go to the funeral. To show respect, Caleb said, because they had few friends to speak of. Never visited and were seldom visited. Pearl had been up for so long that they never opened the coffin. I wondered if the goiter had died with her or if, like Caleb said he had heard-say, it would feed off of her body down to the bone. Same as a river eel would an old fish. I kept my eyes on Thanie, not knowing what to expect. The preacher preached for the souls of those gathered around and to help Thanie in her grief. But if Thanie was grieving, she never showed it. Fact is, she showed nothing. I heard some gathered there say that Thanie was too numb to feel. They also wondered what she would do now that Pearl was gone. They wondered what could she do. Pearl was all she had ever known. They had buried the thing that was closest to her. I overheard one say that Thanie was too childlike to stay in the house alone. Yet no one figured Thanie would ever leave.

And she didn't. She took up sitting on the porch in the chair Pearl had used. If she wasn't there, she was sitting at the grave.

I wondered if Thanie would ever return to the creek hoping that the man she had left there might hear of Pearl's death and return. But, then, if Caleb had been right about drifters and he had been one, his return was not likely. Although I sat nights to watch, Thanie never came.

Once when I saw her at the creek getting water, it pleased me when she asked if I had caught the mink. I hoped she would invite me to the house, but she never did. She had changed so much I hardly knew her.

When winter had ended and the trees were in bud, I saw Thanie walking down the creek toward our house. When she reached the edge of the yard she stopped, motioning for Ma to meet her there. I hid at the edge of the woodshed to listen, but it ended up being nothing more than a stop to pass a word or two. Thanie was going into Sourwood, and Ma said she thought that would be good for her. To get out. And that if she needed help bringing anything back she would send me with her. She wouldn't.

And that was that, until later in the day when Caleb came home. Coaxing me off out of Ma's hearing, he told me that he had seen Thanie go into Harold Galloway's jewelry store and come out sticking something down inside her bosom. What, he didn't know.

After a few days, I began to forget about it. Even doubted that Caleb had seen it. Ma said Caleb would make up and spread rumors. I believed her now.

It must have been at least a month later that Thanie came down the creek and turned toward our yard, where Ma was hanging clothes. Ma had sent me inside for some more clothespins, and, coming out and seeing Thanie, I hid off. Thanie seemed nervous and fidgety. She stopped just inside the edge of the yard, and Ma walked over to where she was.

"I've come to show you something," Thanie said, squinting off like she expected to see someone. Then she stuck her hand out far enough for me to see that she was wearing a ring. "I've been saving my money. I've always wanted a ring, you know."

"I know, honey," Ma said.

And then Thanie squinted off again. "You won't tell Ma, will you?"

She waited for Ma to say something, but instead Ma started crying softly. "No, honey," Ma answered.

Thanie took the ring off and dropped it into her bosom before she skipped off up the creek.

I could hear Ma still crying, softly.

Fourth of July

It was to be my best July fourth celebration in Sourwood ever, especially when it came to the two main events: the "greasy pole" and the "greasy pig." I had laid plans to win them both this year, even coming out ahead of Caleb. But I kept a secret about that.

The truth was, I had started early. To be ready for the greasy pole I had made more trips into Sourwood than you could count, circling the pole like a sorghum mule, sizing it up and, whenever the main road was clear of people, shinnying up it for as far as I thought safe without being seen. There were only two things missing: the pole being greased down with oil and the ten-dollar bill resting on top of it. This year I would not be greedy: I would wait for the others, including Caleb, to climb first, rubbing off most of the oil, and then just at the right time I would shinny up the pole, pluck off the ten, and be the richest boy in Sourwood.

But while the greasy pole only took being smart, the greasy pig took being smart and having a little money to back it up—in my case, enough money for a pack of firecrackers.

Most people around Sourwood considered the greasy pig the main event since it was easier for everyone to participate, especially the women and younger girls who considered it unwomanlike to shinny up a greasy pole with so many men and younger boys around. But as it had turned out, as far back as I could remember the greasy pig was the only event where the winner was seldom if ever known. And for good reason. The event started simple enough: a young shoat that had been hermited off on the mountain until he was as skittish as a cricket in a chicken lot was greased down with oil until he was as slick as a river eel. Then he was turned loose on a screaming crowd with the same thing on everyone's mind: butchering at the first sign of cold weather.

The pig always lost, but to whom only the winner knew for sure. Because of three reasons, mostly: speed, grease, and greed. The speed of the pig, the grease that kept you slipping off, and the greed that caused someone in the crowd to knock you loose if you ever got a good hold. At his first chance the pig turned toward the river and into the trees. He would hardly be out of sight before you'd hear a gun go off, or maybe two, or maybe three. The winner would be sitting in the forks of a cotton bloom willow using the light of the moon and lights from the celebration, and there were always too many people there to know who was missing.

I had laid my plans for the greasy pig starting out grubbing blackberry vines and sassafras sprouts off the mountain in back of Len Alley's place to help enough grass to take root for his milk cow to graze. He paid me twenty cents a day and I quit after five days, since the pack of firecrackers I needed cost a dollar. My plans were to start the fireworks early this year, well before the pig had time to make it inside the willows. And while the crowd was busy trying to see who was doing the shooting, I planned to scatter some sand on that pig and throw a loop of string around his legs before you could say jackrabbit. The only danger was that someone in the crowd could get itchy and take a shot himself. But I figured that a boy wouldn't be apt to do that, and having so many kids around would stop the olders. As Caleb had said many times, there was always some danger whenever something was to be gained on the other end.

It did bother me, though, especially when the Fourth of July was so close, that Caleb talked so little about it. Generally, he talked every year about how, if we followed his plans, we would end up winning. Though we never had. Always the night before he was as chatty as a jaybird, which brought a scolding from Ma because we weren't sleeping. And it always ended up with our pledging as blood brothers to share both the money and the pig.

But not this year. Even the night before, Caleb climbed into bed and lay there solemn as a stump. Finally, I heard him snoring. But there would be no snoring for me this night: my secret had swelled my eyes until they were as large as Ma's biscuits.

When daylight came Caleb and I were in Sourwood milling around with the people already gathered and watching families drive in on wagons pulled by mules. Many of the men went over near the riverbank to help clear a place for square dancing and set up a platform for the Sourwood Mountain Boys to sit on while they made the music. The women mostly fought the younger kids, trying to keep them away from the river and out of mischief. It was easy to see that the women were losing again this year, what with kids being quicker than greasy pigs and louder when caught.

We milled around until we got hungry in the afternoon, searched for a patch of shade, and ate the biscuit and jelly sandwiches we had brought from home. Shortly after, the band struck up a hoedown, and many in the crowd broke up in foursomes. Just this side of dark would come the greasy pole contest; just the other side of dark, the greasy pig, which the founders of the celebration had believed would make the chase more exciting. I slipped off to the river, got me a pocket full of sand that I planned to use on the pig, and spent the rest of my time watching the band and the men who slipped off from the crowd now and then to get a drink at one of the wagons. I saw Caleb talking to Molly Perkins and thought that his taking a sparking to the girls would make my plans easier when the time came. I'd probably not see him again until we met at the greasy pole.

But we didn't meet there. I looked for him. Surely Molly couldn't mean that much! Well, I thought, that means one less to grab the pole when the time is right. And so I stood close and patted my pocket now and then to make sure I hadn't lost the pack of firecrackers hid there.

The steel pole was no more than twenty feet tall, but with a ten-dollar bill on top it seemed a hundred. It stood close enough to Doc Dinkle's office to reach out with a foot and touch the bricks of the building. The top of the pole was no more than two feet from the top of the roof.

I watched man after man and boy after boy shinny a few feet up the pole to the cheering and heehaws of the others waiting their turn. It took almost an hour for enough oil to be pants-wiped from the pole for anyone to make it over halfway. I moved in closer when Slim Barker made it less than five feet from the top. When Randy Perkins got within two, I made my move.

I never even reached the pole. My dream of owning a ten-dollar bill ended up with my fighting for my life to keep my britches on. Lester Crank, who had the longest arms in Sourwood, had latched his big hands under my belt and, yanking me away, pulled my britches down far enough to bring heehaws from the crowds, shaming me something terrible. Once he let go, he cut in ahead of me and shinnied the pole like a squirrel.

Three-quarters up the pole the loudest yell of the evening went up from the crowd. But not for Lester. All eyes were looking now ahead of him. A pair of hands were reaching over Doc Dinkle's roof, the head of their owner hidden by a feed sack. Inching farther over the flat roof, the hands were closer now to the ten-dollar bill.

Seeing the pointing fingers of the men below, Lester looked toward the top of the pole. He fought the pole, lunging and fighting now to get the hands. The crowd became angry, and while everyone wanted the ten dollars for himself, we all cheered Lester on. At least we'd have a chance later to try to skin him out of it. But just as he reached for the money the fingers from the roof plucked the bill from the pole, and it disappeared over the edge of the roof like a green bird.

"Egod, lynch 'im!" someone yelled, and the crowd turned into a mob.

They busted in poor Doc Dinkel's door, climbed the stairs to the top floor, and pried open the hatch that led to the roof. Standing on shoulders, they hoisted men to the roof. We stood below and waited.

After a short while Harvey Pucket peeped down and said, "He's got away. Jumped along the roofs of buildings like a squirrel crossing out!"

I milled around listening to men quarrel. How they would lynch whoever it was if he could be caught and swearing that next year they'd have the roof guarded. Lester was stopping anyone who would listen, telling them how he had been done in. He never bothered to mention how he had pulled my britches down far enough to expose enough of me to the crowd to keep me dodging for days. I turned toward the river to be alone until it was time for the greasy pig. Half of my plan had been snuffed out by someone who had had a better plan than me.

It was near the river that I found Caleb, tucked up in the shadows of a giant willow. He was so busy with something that I was upon him before he jerked a hand into a pocket. But not quick enough for me to miss what he had tucked away there: a ten-dollar bill. I swallowed and looked around like a thief myself. But we were alone.

"It was you!" I whispered.

Caleb squinted and crossed a finger over his mouth to hush me.

"Will a dollar keep a secret?" he said.

And knowing that Caleb was bad to keep a promise, in fact never remembering him ever keeping one, I said, "Cash it and pay me now!"

"And get me strung up," he said. "Your only brother!"

Knowing if he got away with it I would be as broke as I was now, I said, "Pay me!"

"Not here," Caleb said. "I can't cash it here. I mean everyone knows I ain't got that kind of money. Fact is, they know I ain't got any money at all."

"Pay up," I said.

"Not here!" Caleb said.

"Then where?"

Caleb studied for a moment, scratching his head. Finally, he said, "Across the river."

"Across the river?"

"I'll cash it in one of the saloons close to the river on the West Virginia side."

And so off we went. Caleb, afraid to cross the car bridge carrying so much money, afraid of being seen, chose the railroad bridge, a narrow, dangerous crossing. It was tight walking for fear of meeting a train and having to hang over the side.

"Just don't look down!" he cautioned but didn't need to.

The buildings on the West Virginia point were close enough to the Sourwood River to hear the hum of the current against snags. All saloons, Caleb said.

He chose the second building because it was poorly lit up. Just enough light to read the sign overhead: MADAM SOPHIE'S DEW DROP INN. After Caleb had looked around to see that we weren't being trailed, I followed him inside.

A fat woman sat at a small table under a single, dim light, beckoning Caleb on.

"Where's the bar?" I whispered.

"Probably behind that door," Caleb whispered back, and hearing what sounded like giggles I thought he must be right.

Caleb stepped in front of the fat woman and pulled out the ten-dollar bill. But before he could ask for change she plucked it from him and stuck it down her bosom, a place from which you just knew there was no return. At the same time she tapped a little bell with the palm of her other hand, and two women made their way toward us—painted women, I had heard Ma call them whenever we had seen them outside the saloons in Sourwood when the town was wet under local option.

"Starting young, ain't you, honey?" the fat woman leaned over and said to Caleb.

By this time the painted women had reached us, and the fat woman looked at them and said, "Paid."

Then one of the women reached down and pinched me on the cheek. "Is this my little peckerwood?" she said.

I blinked from fear, and when I opened my eyes I saw that Caleb was making a dead run for the door. We met there, bumping one another as we passed through.

We made our way over the riverbank, caught by bugleweed and scratched by briars and snags, and dived into the river, swimming like wild ducks toward the Kentucky shore. Reaching the bank, we climbed out like half-drowned rats. Caleb held his head to one side trying to shake water out of an ear.

I reached for my pocket that held the firecrackers. I pulled them out, and the powder from inside the wrappings dripped like grey mud. "My firecrackers are ruined!" I said. I had lost my chance for the greasy pig too.

But Caleb never answered. He glanced quickly back over the river as if he were being followed and disappeared into the willows. Halfway up the bank, I passed him!

A Pair of Shoes

I had gone into Kelsey Stumbo's hardware store in Sourwood for two reasons. One, I wanted to figure the cost of line and hooks needed to run a trotline from the mouth of the Sourwood River to just this side of the tip of the West Virginia point. With work scarce around Sourwood, and blackberries that I picked now in the hot July sun fetching no more than ten cents a gallon, I needed a job in the worst way, which made for my second reason. Caleb had heard that Kelsey was looking for a boy to tar the roof on his store and said I might get the job if I got there early. Caleb had hooked him a job for the summer with Bates Riley raising garden produce along the rich bottoms of Sourwood Creek and peddling it around Sourwood by horse and wagon, which made fair money and a steadier job. Then, too, Bates was a gospel man except when it came to the price of produce and work payment, but easier to work for than Kelsey Stumbo. Not as bad to hawk you while you worked. For it was well known that nothing and nobody suited Kelsey, including himself. He would skin you for a penny and run you off over a bull nickel.

"Get there early enough and you might get lucky," Caleb said.

"Go myself except I promised Bates I'd make the summer and fall with him even though the work is harder and all and the end of every third row of whatever you're working or picking cost you a verse of scripture, being a gospel man, you know."

"Scripture ain't going to hurt you none," I said, throwing in something I heard Ma say and to temper the lie he had just told. I mean, not telling the whole of it. That Bates's daughter Tisha worked in the fields too and had already taken the place of trotlines and bluetick hounds with him. She was all he talked about now. Tisha and the picture show when his nerve was strong enough to ask and get around Bates for taking her to a house of sin.

I was early enough. The fog had not yet been burned off over the town and the smell of the river was everywhere. But judging the wind playing in the cotton willows nearby, I knew the wind and an early sun would burn it off.

I was caught up in my dreams of a trotline, of sitting in the warm sand along the river tying niblines and stringing them along the trotline every three feet, to be baited with fat yellow grasshoppers that I would catch in the horseweed patches along the river. I bumped into Eunis Alley just as I reached the hardware store. He came out of the store carrying a box under one arm and had a smile on his face as broad as the distance between two niblines. Walking independent-like, he stopped at the wooden bench Kelsey kept outside his store for specials he claimed to have from time to time but that, rumor was, he hadn't sold for so long that no one remembered. Eunis squinted toward the store to see if Kelsey was watching before he propped a bare foot upon the bench, knowing what Kelsey might do if he caught a boy doing that. I didn't see Kelsey in sight either but did notice a ladder leaned against the downriver side of the big two-story building, the last rung and two sides of the ladder sticking above the rim of the roof like a slingshot fork. The building had a wide, flat roof with just enough slope for runoff.

Eunis crooked me over, and when I got there, he raised dust

with a spurt of tobacco, man-like but whipping-like if his ma knew
it.

"What's up with you today?" Eunis asked.

"Trotline and a job Caleb heard that Kelsey might have for
tarring the roof of his building," I answered.

Eunis studied that, raising another cloud of dust with ambeer.

"Trotline might be a go if you got the money to make one,"
he answered, "but the job ain't."

"How come?" I asked, looking to make sure Kelsey would not
see Eunis raise the dust with ambeer and lay some of the blame on
me. For spitting in front of his store, among other things, was something he didn't take lightly to; not even among the old men who
came to whittle of the summer when a sale wasn't on and the bench
in use. They had to buy the plug twist from him but bring their
own cans to spit in and carry away when they left at the end of the
day.

Instead of answering my question, Eunis said, "Big trotline?
Long and nib-full?"

Catching a chance for a brag, I looked independent myself
and important-like and said, "Tip of the West Virginia point."

"Take a heap of money to run a line that far," he answered.
"How you figure to do that? Pick berries until the sun dries them
up and you ain't got enough to buy that much line."

What Eunis didn't know was that I had sold off enough berries already to pay for half the trotline and was figuring the job
from Kelsey to cover the rest. What I had now was between me
and my pocket. For I had learned the hard way that money was
something you never bragged about to the likes of Caleb or Eunis
or the older boys, especially since they had long since stopped bragging about fishing and hound dogs to talk about girls and what
was playing at the picture show. They were all bad to want to borrow on the strength of a payback with extra but left you with a no-
catch and bare hook. With a girl on the end, they were good at
sweet talk. It had worked on me before, their throwing in trotlines,

deep-chested blueticks, redbones, black and tans, and the sort to soften me; playing on my curiosity about the girls to boot. Eunis, like Caleb, was better at talking than working.

I said, "I figure to pick me up a job from Kelsey tarring his roof."

Eunis hitched the box he was carrying tighter under his arm. He said, "Too late on that."

"How come?" I asked.

"I already got the job," he answered, staring off and then judging the wind with a wet finger. "Just waiting for the fog to lift and the sun to heat the tin so the tar will spread. Might be ready now. Kelsey wants it finished today this side of a rain he says could be building." And then, as if he knew all there was to know about tar when I was sure he knew no more than me but had heard it from Kelsey, he added, "Spreads better in the heat of the sun, you know. Streaks in damp weather."

I thought once of doubling back on what he had said, mocking with Kelsey's voice to do so, something I had become more than good at. Both me and Caleb had learned during nights pretending to be asleep and looking for mischief without Ma or Pa hearing. Mocking Kelsey and others was a natural, especially Kelsey, since he had chased away every boy in town for little or nothing more times than you could count—for being too slow in delivering a package of something he had sold or in helping him set merchandise back inside when the mule wagons came into Sourwood on Saturdays, mules being second only to boys in picking around on specials on the wooden bench. And he got by with it mostly, when it came to boys. He whipped with words and a cane that never met its mark but left wind-sounds of how close it had been. Outrunning him was a brag but risky.

Maybe it was seeing the look on my face and my want of a trotline. I'll never know. But Eunis said, "Big roof." He squinted toward the sky again. "Rain could be closer than it looks." He looked now toward the ladder leaned against the roof. "Big roof," he said again.

Disgusted that I had lost the job, I answered, "What's it mean to me?"

"Means that it could be I might be looking around for a little help on the roof," he said, surprising me. "Could be I might be wanting to finish today too being as how it's Friday and the picture show opens tomorrow." He tucked at the box again. "Could be I got something special in mind. Could pay up to half what Kelsey is paying me."

"How much is that?" I asked, knowing there was little chance of getting the truth of it, but that he might say before thinking.

Eunis never answered that. Instead, he lifted his bare foot off the bench and scratched his big toe around in the dust, uncovering a few willow shavings left by the old men, a cut of chewed tobacco called "dead man," and an emptied Golden Grain Tobacco pouch. He worked his foot and his mouth to help his toe until he was able to hook the loop of string used to pull closed the opening of the sack. He wiggled it like a worm, checking to make sure Kelsey could not be seen through the glass door. While I watched, I worried about the job Eunis offered to me. For Eunis, I knew, was like Caleb on something of this sort. Taking a job with him, you'd end up doing all the work and reaping none of the pay. But the greed for the trotline was strong. He might pay. This could be the time. People could change, I had heard Ma say. Even boys, she claimed. Miracles did happen.

Biding time to think, I said, "What's the picture show got to do with it?"

Eunis squinted like he thought someone might hear whatever he intended to say. He spurted ambeer again, pushing both of our luck to the brim.

"That's a secret," he answered.

I thought about that. How a secret could egg you on, keep you around the hook. For a secret held magic while it lasted, mysterious and exciting. But I also knew that a secret was for telling, not keeping. With only time in between. Remembering how it was with Caleb on secrets, I figured Eunis would keep his until he got me on the roof. No matter. What he had in the box and had not said was hard enough. I tried to hold out.

"I don't know," I said. "It's a big roof. Take all day and maybe then some. I had my mind set to be on the river and go with a shorter trotline if the job didn't work out for full pay."

Eunis lifted his foot to the bench again, tempting fate no farther away than Kelsey was from the front door of his store. He fondled the box in his hands, set it on his knee. He lifted a corner of the box and squinted inside. Then he just looked off like what he had seen there was nothing at all and said, "Half of what Kelsey pays would buy a lot of hooks and line. Wouldn't take all day, either. The two of us there."

My eyes were glued to the box now, my mind a part of it. I made the mistake of turning curiosity loose. "What's in the box?" I asked.

Setting the hook, Eunis answered, "Secret number two. Help me tar the roof before sundown and find out."

I said, "Promise?" wondering why I had said that. I mean, a promise being a nothing to nowhere.

And then with words sweet enough for bees to work, he said, "You got my word." Just like gospel. That the river would run backwards was a better bet.

Blinded by the chance for money and two secrets, I said, "I'll do it!"

And we turned around the side of the building that held the leaning ladder. A bucket of tar was on the ground beside it.

"You carry the bucket of tar up the ladder," he said. "I'll need my free hand to hold the secret in the box."

And then, on what was promising to be the hottest day of the year, I picked up a bucket of tar heavy as a sack of feed and struggled up the rungs toward the top of the ladder, inching my way like a measuring worm; a worm that, superstition told here on the mountain, dropped on you and, caught inching, was measuring your funeral box. I squinted through the sun at Eunis up ahead of me carrying the secret in the box as carefully as he would a poke of loose eggs.

Pulling ourselves over the rim of the roof, Eunis quickly made his way to the shadows cast by the chimney and carefully laid the box inside the shadows like the heat from the sun would be apt to harm whatever was inside, something alive. For the spare of a moment I thought I would have tarred the roof for the secret of the box alone but was grateful that Eunis did not know that. I wiped the sweat that broke all over me now, especially over my eyes. This was to be the scorcher of scorchers! I watched the box for a movement.

Once settled in, I tiptoed back to the edge of the roof to see if Kelsey was in sight, had come to check on us. The two of us! For it had been Eunis who had done the hiring on me, not Kelsey. Kelsey didn't know. And I thought again how grouchy Kelsey was when it came to boys; how he said boys set their minds to lazying their lives away on the mountain or the rivers and always wanted twice as much for work as they were worth. I remembered too how bad he was said to be, by Caleb and others who had worked for him, about checking on you and your work. Cussing you out, he took the time off it took him to do it and charged it to you as loafing off. If caught on the roof, two things might work in my favor. One was that Caleb had said he wanted the roof tarred the worst you could imagine, since it leaked during the last rain and he had lost some items, had to mark them down for special sale. Two, another rain was close. Not seeing Kelsey in sight, I tiptoed back to the other side of the roof, the side where we would begin the tarring. Eunis had knelt, trying to pry open the lid of the can that held the tar. He stared off at the box and then at me. He caught me staring.

"Curious?" he asked.

Not wanting to seem too anxious, afraid of what it could cost me, I answered, "Maybe."

Eunis glanced around the roof like he was expecting to see

someone there. And then, seeing nothing but the sky and the roof around us, he scooted across to the chimney where the box was and cracked the lid again.

"Whoeeeeeeee!" he said, loud enough for me to hear but not, I hoped, for anyone below.

I felt my heart flutter.

"Afraid it might get away?" I whispered.

Eunis frowned. "What'll get away?" he asked, louder than I thought he ought.

"What you got in the box," I whispered.

Eunis laughed, again too loud. "Ain't apt to," he said.

"How come?" I asked, figuring he might make a mistake and tell like you do sometimes on a secret too exciting to keep penned up.

"Can't run, can't fly," he said. "Just purty." He stared at me. "Think you could keep a secret?"

I swallowed. I would have tarred the roof single-handed to know. Who knew what would follow? Maybe his secret had grown too much to keep.

"Sure can," I answered. But never had before.

And then he reached inside the box and I jumped back, fairly expecting something to jump or fly out. Disappointed, I watched him pull out a pair of shoes. He matched them against the blue sky and squinted at me.

"Part of my pay for tarring the roof," he said, almost too excited to talk. "Brand new! Lucked into them minutes before Kelsey put them out on the bench for a special. Why, they wouldn't have been there long enough to make a shadow! How lucky can I be!"

Good golly! I thought. *Only a pair of shoes.* What a secret I had fallen for—had wanted to fall for. I had my mind made up that he had captured a wild varmint or something of the sorts, not a pair of black leather shoes age-cracked, high buttoned, and pointed toed. Kelsey had probably had them since the day he opened the store years ago, shoes being a specialty item. He had only sold a single pair that any of us could remember, or rather, had traded them for work, actually. To Arlie Spurlock, who put them on inside the store just this side of a rain but got caught in a downpour before he was home. Well, when the water hit the shoes the bottoms peeled from the tops like peeling pawpaws, and Arlie left footprints in the mud with his bare feet the rest of the way home, the shoe tops bouncing up and down on his ankles like lids on boiling pots.

"It ain't nothing but shoes!" I said, louder than I should have.

"Wrong as usual," Eunis said, catching the sound of my voice. "Not just shoes, but specials! The only pair like 'em in Sourwood."

"Why did you hide them in the box?" I asked, mad mostly since hiding them there was what caught and cost me.

"These are stealing shoes!" he said, squinting off like someone was near enough to snatch them now. "I couldn't gamble with me having to lay them up before I could get them home!"

He put the shoes back inside the box and placed the box back in the shade. He pulled a stiff brush from his back pocket and a wood shingle cut from a piece of cedar to stir the tar. Remembering that he had said the shoes were a part of the pay for tarring the roof and being as how I hadn't started work yet, I said, "You said part pay."

"I did and that's a fact," he answered. "Got the shoes and two dollars to boot. Help me with the roof and this money's yours."

With one secret gone and doubt about the money, I said, "Shoes!"

Eunis grinned. "And girls!" he answered, giving away secret number two.

"Girls?" I asked, thinking how much Eunis was like Caleb on being able to weave a girl into everything we did or talked about.

"Well," Eunis said, "mostly one girl now." He squinted off. "Keep another secret?"

"I guess so," I answered, knowing that he was going to tell me now anyway and then talk about it until the roof was tarred.

"It's Katie Crank," he whispered.

I didn't have the heart to tell him she was the same girl all the boys had their eyes on and the one Caleb said would promise the moon. A promise with no show, whatever that meant.

"Didn't figure it would matter much to you," he said, looking off reckless-like. "Leastways not yet. I mean, your life still being trotlines, joeboats, and hound dogs. Way I was once, and never knew how well off it all was back then. I mean, no girl to think about. Like how many other boys are eyeing the same girl. Lose a trotline to high water and you set another; lose a girl to another boy what's found means to get her a picture show and it could be forever. See her the first time, down on fishing; see her again, down on hunting; see her again, and throw in the dog!" He looked out over the roof. "Girls are exciting and miserable!"

"Why you fooling with them?" I asked, having asked Caleb the same thing many times, with no answer that settled curiosity.

"Don't rightly know," he answered. "It's like the urge to fish and hunt, only stronger, having a pairing-off about it like making nests and digging holes."

I asked, "What's girls got to do with shoes?"

"Simple," he answered. "They won't go to a picture show with you barefooted!" He looked back at the bucket. "We better get started if I aim to have time to get off this roof with my shoes and get over to Katie's to see about the movie on Saturday."

"What makes you think the shoes will work?" I asked.

"Something about being shoed-up that turns 'em on," he said. "No telling! I mean, I'll be the only boy in Sourwood with a pair like these. Got 'em just this side of the bench. It's my lucky day. You figure my luck!"

I didn't plan to. I mean, I had got myself hooked on tarring a roof by two secrets that weren't worth telling and for a price that might never have been offered. To boot, I'd got myself penned on a hot roof listening to girl-talk all day. What I had to do now was to steer him off girls and on to trotlines, to make life barely livable and hope that he was telling the truth on the money.

And then, watching him spread the tar, I got to thinking that I might not want to get him off girl-talk at all. How girl-talk might even turn me a favor like it did on Caleb from time to time. Especially remembering the times when Caleb and I were cutting and cording wood and my payment was listening to him talk about girls. Egging him on and watching him take his spite out on the wood as a payback to someone who had cut him out and got the girl ahead of him. Nodding to show him how sad and mournful that all was. In the end he seldom remembered that he had done all the work while I had lazied and listened. Dreamed off on fishing and hound dogs while he got worked up over some girl that flittered from flower to flower. Listening to dreams that never worked out but were exciting now and then to hear, which I took for boot. Now and then trying to break into the conversation to talk about fishing just to throw him off but coaxing him on.

I thought that it might work on Eunis. He was as anxious to take Katie to the picture show as I was to get to the river with enough line and hooks to reach the tip of the point. If it worked, maybe I'd get a little money for listening and chalk it all up to payback time. Some things seemed to be in my favor: the name of the girl and the shoes in the box to remind him of what was up front.

I scooted to where he was brushing the tar, feeling the hot tin on the soles of my feet. Unbearable! "Pretty is she?" I whispered. "I mean, Katie."

He lifted the brush, and I watched the soft tar run down the handle onto his arm like black molasses. His eyes were full of sweat, and he tried to stay on his knees to keep the hot tin from burning his feet.

"Hush your mouth!" he said, but grinning. "Like a speckled pup." He touched the brush to the tin, harder. "She's prettier than pretty!"

The brush became a blur now, and I knew that Eunis was on his way, maybe even greedier over a girl than Caleb. I eased over near the shade from the chimney as sparse as it was and tried to make myself comfortable. I could pull up the trotline in my mind now and throw in something to Eunis whenever he slowed down. He was wrapped up in Katie, trying to hum a song with a voice that sounded as squeaky as dry oarlocks. I tried to make hearing it bearable by pulling up my dreams and glancing toward the river. I saw him slowing down.

"You think the shoes will do it, huh?" I whispered.

It was like pulling a starter cord on a chainsaw. He dipped and spread and hummed like a jaybird. Once he let out an oath that would have got us both whipped but made him more grownupitish and the sort. I even thought I'd try that oath myself whenever I was sure Ma was out of hearing and Caleb wouldn't tell or hold it over me.

The tar was mixing with his feet, and I watched it ooze between his toes. He flinched from the heat. He grinned and made the most of it. I had to give him credit for that. He puckered his mouth. I knew the tar was burning his feet.

"Now wouldn't I be a purty thing going over there with the tar on my feet and asking her to take in a show with me?" he chuckled. "Or being shed of the tar but crusted with dirt and a stubbed toe." He frowned to show the worth of that. "No! We finish here on this roof and I'll shed my feet of the tar and traipse over there with my new shoes! Now you just stand back and . . ."

To add more coals to a burning fire I stopped him short of what he had intended to say, taking into account that I had noticed the size of the shoes and thought at the time they were the longest I had ever seen.

"I love my shoes," he added pitiful-like.

"Think the shoes will fit all right?"

"Paper in the ends will cheat the length if they don't," he answered. "First new pair I ever owned."

I watched him now, thinking how silly it was that he had let a girl bake his feet on a hot tin roof. It occurred to me that I ought to scoot near the edge of the roof and peer over just in case Kelsey decided to check on how things were going. I had heard old men talking from where the bench was and knew they had come to whittle. I caught Kelsey's voice among theirs now and again. I looked at Eunis. He must have seen the worry on my face. He said, "Scoot over and look at the old men if you want."

I did. And good thing, too, I thought. I saw Kelsey turn from the front of the store and head toward the ladder. I followed him with my eyes, scooting along the edge of the roof, and watched his hands touch the first rung. He was coming up to check, I thought.

I hurried over and took the brush from Eunis like I was intending to rest him for a spell. He slid himself to the splinter of chimney shade just as Kelsey peered over the roof and saw me spreading tar. Before Kelsey could say anything, Eunis said, "Got me some help." He stared off toward the sky. "Got to figuring two could get ahead of a rain better than one. About how a rain will streak and all."

Kelsey shielded his eyes from the blistering sun. "Well," he said, "rain is chancy but boys more so. One might work, but get two together and they go to acting like boys. But since you're both up here I'll chance it. But if I catch either one of you loafing on this roof today there'll be hell to pay! And another thing: the payment's the same!"

Once he had disappeared down the ladder I handed Eunis the brush and said, "Pretty sure she'll go to the show when you ask?"

And Eunis tarred into the afternoon telling me why it was that she could not help but go. How it was a girl shucked up to importance and took up with them that had something the others didn't have. Like new shoes. The chimney was casting thinner shadows, and the sun was the hottest I could remember. I tried to shield my feet. I watched poor Eunis tar and wondered how he could hold up with nothing on the end of the brush but tar and a dream. I wondered how his bare feet could stand the hot tin, almost hot

enough to burn the flesh as black as the tar. His overalls were covered with it and his face was streaked where he had tried to wipe
the sweat away. I felt sorry for him while I searched for shade.

Late afternoon I heard the talk pick up down at the bench
and scooted out of the shade to take another look. Lazying around
on the roof had made me restless. But not enough to tar. I peeked
over and saw Kelsey talking to Ed Randall. I closed off my ear that
faced Eunis's girl talk so that I could catch what they were saying,
cupping my hand to the other ear making a morning glory horn.
My heart skipped a beat over what I heard.

"Like I say," Kelsey said, "one boy might work but two will
loaf. They ain't weaned off nowadays like me and you once was,
Ed. Too quiet up there to suit me. I'd better check shortly."

I scooted back across the roof, careless enough to smear tar
on me by the time I reached Eunis. I whispered, "You've been at it
a long time now, Eunis. Why don't you ease over to the shade from
the chimney and rest a spell."

Eunis squinted at me in a daze from work and sun. It had put
the drowsies to him. His eyes showed it. Rendered by the heat, he
wiped his forehead and scooted across the roof to the chimney,
leaving a streak of tar to show his path.

Once inside the thin shadow cast now by the chimney, he
pulled the box close to his chest, stretched out on his back, closed
his eyes, and was snoring, his head against the brick chimney. Worn
out from work, sapped by heat, but with a smile on his face and
probably dreams inside his head, though Caleb said there was not
room for much there. But what Eunis had lost up there had gone
to muscle, in the arms mostly, making him stronger than most of
the lot of them and bad to fight. Everyone I knew had heard-say
on things like that. How, if you lost a leg, the strength of it crossed
to the other leg; eyes, ears, and arms would do the same thing.
Sometimes you got a little extra like Eunis had, because whatever
he had lost out of his brain had been aplenty, more than usual.
Maybe there was room now for the shoes, Katie, and to knock my

head off, given reason. Being smart, Caleb said his own head was fuller than most, no room left.

Knowing that Kelsey was on his way up the ladder and that he hadn't checked the roof since early morning, I got to spreading tar faster than a rumor. By the time he reached the top and pulled himself over the rim of the roof, I looked worn out. He glanced at me and then quickly caught Eunis with his eyes, snoring and peaceful-like beside the chimney. Kelsey crossed his lips with his finger, signaling for quiet, and eased by me bending low as he did so to whisper, "Been there all day?" he asked.

And for shame, I nodded my head yes, sad-like and overworked. Poor Eunis, I remembered thinking, as Kelsey sneaked toward him, mad as a wet hen. And for shame again, I thought how glad I was it was Eunis there now instead of me, though it had been my resting and cooling-off place the livelong day.

I got scared thinking about what Kelsey might do, throw him off the roof or something. It was a long way down, and although I figured Eunis's head could probably take it better than most being cushioned by empty space, it was still a high fall. Maybe with luck, Eunis would hear Kelsey in time and make it down the ladder before being caught. It was too unbearable to watch but too exciting not to. And then, without intending, I coughed and caught a quick glance from Kelsey that told me I might have to pay later. Eunis's eyes popped open, and, born to run, he turned loose of the box and slid toward the chimney. Kelsey went after him but fell on the slick tar. Eunis reached the ladder, sliding like a muskrat down a slide, with Kelsey above, stomping to reach Eunis's fingers holding the rungs. Once on solid ground, Eunis ran off into a tall, thick horseweed patch in back of the building, with Kelsey yelling words that may have scorched all of Sourwood.

Winded and mad, he squinted back at the ladder and walked toward it with a you're-next look on his face. To make matters worse, the old men who had been whittling at the bench had seen it all. Sicking Kelsey on like it was a dog chase, slapping their knees.

The louder they slapped and yelled, the madder Kelsey got. They stopped when Eunis disappeared into the horseweeds, knowing the chase was over on that end.

I saw Kelsey touch the rungs of the ladder and start his climb. I thought of jumping but didn't. It was too high up! With my luck, he'd catch me on the way down and skin me out in front of the old men, who would be cheering him on like it was a chicken fight. With the only hope I had, I grabbed the tar brush and went to tarring as fast and furious as I knew how. I worked like I had one thing now in mind, to get the roof tarred before a rain. Working for nothing. I figured I would be throwing in the money I had made on berries.

But that was before I saw the smile on Kelsey's face when he squinted over the top of the ladder. "Had to do it all yourself, eh?" Kelsey said.

For shame, I shook my head yes.

"Well," Kelsey said, "he hooked me too. Hooked me for a pair of shoes fresh off the paddlewheel boat up from Louisville." Kelsey was squinting now, gauging the roof, the amount of work done and work left. I was glad that he probably couldn't see much of the backside beyond the chimney and toward the riverside, which hadn't been tarred at all. Maybe thinking to help us both, he said, "But, don't worry. I'll catch 'im! He'll be coming through town again and I'll be waiting! With more than reason enough. First off, he hooked me for a pair of shoes ready for a special; hooked you with a roof to tar alone; made a laughing stock out of me in front of the old men with only one thing more important to them than seeing who among them can cut the longest shaving without its breaking, and that's to spread a rumor. Worse than old women on that! Mark that down to remember! Old men. He'll pay dearly!"

I was so scared now that I worked while he talked hoping to pick up any favor I could. It seemed to work. He watched me swish the brush and shook his head favor-like. He was too big to get around, and I was too high up to jump, too little to fight. Life was miserable, and maybe short! He turned back toward the ladder, which pleased me. I worked harder, pretending I was too busy to be watching him. But I saw him hoist a leg over the rim of the building and set it on the first rung of the ladder. He started disappearing slowly, sinking out of sight like a fish sinker with a blue-sky-water background. And then, with only his head above the roof, he said, "The shoes are yours!"

I swallowed, wondering if I had heard him right and what he thought that meant to me, shoes as old as the mountains, four sizes too big and nothing on my mind but trotlines! With what he had said being too much for me to keep inside, I said, louder than I ought, "Shoes?"

"Shoes," Kelsey repeated, leaving no mistake. "That's what the payment was for tarring. My agreement with Eunis. You did the work, the shoes are yours. To keep. Unless you want to keep a shoe with Eunis getting the other to wear at his funeral when I catch him!" And then he squinted again over the roof. "I'll say this, took some work on your part to get all this done. You finish, no need to come by and spread tar on the ground in front of the store; I got a special coming up tomorrow. Tar's bad to come off and hold on."

And that was that. All day on the roof and with nothing to show but a pair of shoes! Shoes so big that on my feet it would be like a sparrow stepping in an eagle's nest. And wearing shoes was the furthest thing from my mind. First off, I'd be laughed off the mountain, with Caleb leading the pack. And Eunis? He'd snuff me out! The shoes were closer than a girl to him.

It was first things first. With Kelsey the closest, and figuring I had better finish the roof by dark, I started back to work. Sweat and tar covered my face, and my eyes burned from salt and tar, but not nearly as much as my feet. They were almost blistered. The sun was unbearable, like it had no intentions of ever setting this day. I tried to get my burning feet out of my mind. I thought of Eunis, wondering how far he had run before feeling safe enough to stop and catch his breath. If he had run all the way to the river and hid-off on the point, which I probably would have done with the likes of Kelsey after me and knowing what hung at the end of a catch.

In a way, I felt sorry for Eunis. But then, sizing up what part of the roof he had not tarred, a roof that seemed to be growing ahead of the tar brush now, I took that back and faulted him for loafing. But mostly I thought of the shoes still inside the box by the chimney. I knew that wherever Eunis was now, he was think-ing of one thing: shoes. Shoes that he had earned by tarring almost all of the roof—and would have finished tarring what was left if Kelsey hadn't caught him taking a short rest and misjudged and not allowed time to know the opposite. I figured too that Eunis didn't know I knew the shoes were all he had coming for payment. That he had probably planned to lie and say Kelsey had added boot and would make up some amount when he simmered down. Money that he would pass on to me sometime. With little inside his head, he'd think I'd believe that. I mean, who would have thought Kelsey would offer me the shoes, as valuable as Eunis said they were? Especially since he hadn't been the one to hire me in the first place. What work I had done was for nothing, owed by Eunis. Payment, a day lost along the river.

I worried myself right up to the chimney where the shoes were and sat down on the tin, lifting my burning feet into the air to catch wind that had not come high up this day. From where I was, I thought I could see steam coming from the river beyond, a boiling haze in the sun. I thought of the shoes again, still inside the box. To Eunis a girl and a picture show, to me relief for my burning feet!

The day was growing late and the roof larger. I could hear the old whittlers quarreling over the length of shavings and calling for Kelsey to judge. I lifted the shoes from the box like birds out of the nest. I tried to think of things to get what I was thinking about the shoes off my mind. I thought of how Eunis had given blisters for his shoes, how he had left them inside the box to protect them from the tar. It was pitiful-like.

What I *should* have been doing was thinking of how I might get the roof tarred and the shoes back to Eunis, something that might, given hide-out time, pacify Eunis. Instead I was measuring the shoes for my feet. What a nice, thick sole was attached to the bottom of them!

I pretended to wish that I had a last chance to give the shoes to Eunis. But for shame, when I was given the wish, I turned it down as cold as a gravedigger. Caleb would have called it a chance for redemption. It came in the sound of Eunis's pitiful voice seeping out of the horseweed patch at the rear of the building. I edged near the rim of the building, not close enough to be seen from the ground, but close enough to hear better. I cupped a hand to my ear and listened.

"Throw down my shoes," I heard Eunis, a mournful whispering, taking a chance that could get us both snuffed out. I knew now that he had not only not swum the river, but that his love for the shoes had kept him inside the horseweed patch close enough to get caught had Kelsey chosen to brave the chance of snakes and chiggers. It was a love that deserved my making the right choice on what to do; it was a right choice I never took. Instead of thinking of poor Eunis down there hid-off, barely, with a good chance of being caught, I thought of the nights that Caleb and I had spent mocking the voices of others, especially Kelsey's since he often yelled at us when we passed his hardware store, for nothing except that we were boys and not apt to buy.

Twisting my mouth, which was a part of the mock, I said loud enough to carry to where Eunis hid, "I know he'll come back for the shoes! I've got the equalizer waiting for him when he does. He'll not beat me down the ladder this time or see me hid out behind the chimney! Eunis is a short timer!"

I heard him scurrying around inside the horseweeds, breaking down stalks on his way to swimming the river and hiding out along the point. And that was that.

Allowed time, I slipped my feet inside the shoes for relief. I intended to keep the tar on the soles and off the tops, but it never worked out. Slipping and sliding, I could barely recognize that I had shoes on my feet at all, just two big balls of tar. Both inside and out, being the shoes were so big and fit so loose. While my feet no longer burned, the shoes became a burden, heavy and sticking to the tar. The roof grew bigger still and the sun lower. I was too tired to finish the place behind the chimney that could not be seen from the ladder and too tired to outrun Eunis if he caught me on the ground and found out about the shoes. The shoes were now stuck too tight to get off my feet. The way it was, I would be lucky to get down the ladder. My feet were almost too heavy to lift or fit the rungs. And my burden heavier than both: to slip by Kelsey because I had not finished tarring the roof, and to be ahead of Eunis who should be making his way by now back across the river to try for the shoes one last time before dark.

By the time I reached the ground, my legs were so tired that I could little more than shuffle. Add to that, once on the ground the tar on the shoes was gathering everything it touched: sticks, cigar and cigarette butts, dead man chews, leaves, and grass that the tar cropped as close as sheep's teeth. Whatever was there, the shoes claimed and I carried.

By the time I had shuffled to the foot of the mountain, lifting the shoes had become like lifting two river barges with full tow.

This side of dark, I stepped into the shadows of the mountain, certain of one thing: the only way out was to become a hermit.

The Jimson Dog

On Saturday the stern-wheeler *Mattie Wren* blew for a landing at Sourwood, and the whistle settled across the town like a river fog, bringing life to the rumor that had hovered over the town for days: Homer Spurlock, who owned the Sourwood Bank, had bought his wife, Generva, who owned the society in Sourwood, a big high-browed dog the likes of which the town had never seen. A dog too societied to be ciphered by commons, like ones owned by uppities in Cincinnati, Louisville, and as far away as Boston; a showing-off sort that was heard-say to cost as much as a hillside farm. Which was sinful, Ma said, a body paying that kind of money just to show off, with people starving in the world about. And add-to, one that was rumored to be house-kept instead of outside with the fleas. But I had overheard old men of the town say the dog could still be a bargain if it pacified Generva and stilled her long tongue. For it was well talked about how she henpecked poor Homer, which led in turn to his taking it out on customers who came to borrow or float loans. The big dog would come as show and company, company since she had no children of her own. Two rumors followed this: 1) that she figured Sourwood was too back-woodsy to bring a child up in, and 2) that it might grow up to be a woodsrabbit like me, Caleb, and other boys of the town.

Coming by way of Cincinnati, being picked off and married up there while Homer had gone for a bankers meeting, she held little hope for Sourwood being more than a backwoods river town. And so she laid back and watched for ways to educate the town and law boys who stepped on the grass or flowers in her yard, and waited for showboats such as the *Goldenrod* or *Cotton Bloom* to come upriver bringing society music, dancing girls, and shows down at the wharf. Stomping affairs that she made the most of, traipsing down the bank with those from town she had tried to recruit as fit for her society, all dressed for the occasion and joined by others who went out of curiosity, being penned off in Sourwood with little coming in from the outside.

Me and Caleb tried to keep a clear path, but since Ma did her washings, we had to pick up and deliver the wash and took slurs and evil eyes both ways. Ma had little to say about that except that poor folks had a long row to hoe, and that Pa had taken a loan on the shoe shop he operated in Sourwood.

But let that be.

For whatever reason, the big dog was being delivered today, brought up from Cincinnati by Captain Walker and booked as a first-class passenger instead of riding with common baggage. With the dying whistle, the town followed like a river in flood stage that had decided to pull back within its banks.

Before the boat was tied off at the wharf, the crowd had gathered. While most had come to see the dog, the wharfing of a stern-wheeler from downriver always drew a sizable crowd. People came to see what was dropped off, to gossip with the passengers going on upriver to Pittsburgh or elsewhere beyond imagining, and also to pick off any news from downriver. Women dressed out in gingham, some holding babies in their arms while keeping a tight fist on older girls who tugged to stray and whispered gossip and the sort. The men stood farther back, some whittling the soft willow wood and waiting.

I slipped with Caleb and the older boys inside a stand of willow seedlings grown out into the river and waited. I expected to hear Caleb and the boys whisper out of the willows to coax the girls away from their mothers. That's the way it always was whenever we gathered at the river for a stern-wheeler or showboat. I would quarrel that his coaxing was causing me to miss what was being sent from the boat to the shore, and he would tell me that I'd be whispering too whenever I was old enough to know the difference between a girl and a trotline.

Looking around, I saw that Caleb and the rest were eyeing the river as close as me, bypassing the girls. Too curious to whisper, almost too curious to breathe. Afraid we would miss something. Bees were working the blooms of the willows, whirling by in spots of streaked yellow and black bands. I watched Caleb brush a willow top out of the way, giving a wider view. I could not see a single girl trying to slip loose from her mother's grip. All eyes were on the boardwalk being stretched from the deck of the stern-wheeler to the shore. Men threw ropes to tie the boat off while it unloaded, cheating the current trying to pull it downriver.

The world became as quiet as a wind-laid night river. Captain Walker stepped out on the deck holding what had to be the society dog on a leash, so fancy that it caught the glint of the sun and hurt your eyes if you stared. The dog stood there, tall, slick-haired, and black-and-white-spotted as newlights. Its tail stood at high noon as it looked out over the oohs and aahs of the crowd.

When Captain Walker reached down to pat the dog on the head you could hear the growl, loud enough to scare the small children so much that some started to cry. Captain Walker jerked back in time to miss the big dog's teeth with his hand. But his britches leg didn't fare as well. The society dog set its teeth in the cloth and ripped a slit long and wide enough to expose Captain Walker's leg, which was very white being up in the forecastle and little exposed to the sun. Then for no reason I could think of, it growled again and snapped like it was set to draw blood.

"Why would it do that?" I whispered to Caleb.

"Mainly," Caleb whispered back, "a dog that high up in society can do what it wants to."

With the big dog growling and snapping, Captain Walker danced a jig, and the crowd seemed to like that, because, I thought, it was not them dodging the big dog's teeth. But it bothered me. I mean, more than once Captain Walker had bought crawdads from me for a fair price. From Caleb, too. But Caleb, grinning with the others, seemed to have forgotten that. Thinking that if it was me I might just whop the dog on the snout with the handle of the leash, I whispered, "Why is the captain taking that?"

Without changing his sight, Caleb whispered back, "Mainly because like everyone else, he's got a loan at the bank."

Finally the dog let up and wobbled its way down the plank to shore, moving the crowd back like wind at the edge of a hayfield. Not wanting to pay it a favor, I whispered, "Wobbly walking, ain't it?"

"You would be, too, if you had been riding the river all the way upstream from Louisville!" Caleb whispered.

"And it sure ain't no hound dog," I added.

Caleb looked at me with a frown, turning loose a willow top that swung back and hit him across the face keen enough to smart.

"See what you caused!" he said.

I knew that Caleb was over his awe and back to his old self, blaming me for all things that didn't go his way. His old self at least for now.

Funny and strange how it was when the society dog reached shore and Generva took the leash; the dog settled down like everything else that got in her way. They headed upbank with the dog, the crowd parting for them, making a path wide enough to drive a mule wagon through. The big dog stepped high with its paws like it was walking on lily pads, picking its footing.

"Look!" Caleb whispered to me as he pointed to the girls who stood watching, some holding hands over their mouths and cooing like turtle doves. Maybe seeing how it was with the girls watching and making over the big dog with their eyes, he added, "I wouldn't mind being a little society myself."

"How come?" I whispered, remembering the times we talked about how much better off we were to be akin to the rivers and hills, away from society and the sort.

"Mainly," Caleb said, "because I ain't ever been nothing but common for all of my life. Been nowhere, and left with no way of knowing for sure what's up on the other side. But maybe it's like I've heard old-timers say, that the grass is greener over there."

I had heard old-timers say that, too, and had asked Ma about it once. I whispered to Caleb, "Asked Ma about that once, and she said she'd bet a pretty that when you went there you'd find it all picked down. Better to stay at the hole where the fish are biting than to search the rivers and lose fish."

Before the stern-wheeler was out of sight on its way upriver to Pittsburgh, Caleb's world had rendered down to little more than a society dog. In the days that followed, nothing I could say taking away from or adding to the dog made a difference. Hoping to add to, I mentioned the dog making a good tree dog, and Caleb snapped, "A society dog's too high up for varmints! You'll see!"

At nights now, gone was talking ourselves to sleep with plans for the summer along the river. Before the coming of the society dog our plans had been set. We would start early of the mornings when the crocus broke in bloom, fishing for perch that turned out of the bigger but colder Ohio for the warmer water of the Sourwood. Then when the dogwoods were in bloom and the newlights were schooling, we would seine Sourwood Creek for minnows for bait. Of all the fish in the rivers, the newlights brought the best price on the streets of Sourwood. But their run was short lived, and with the coming of summer we turned to catfish, frogs, and turtles. While Ma would eat a turtle, she claimed a frog, having a webbed foot, was akin to scripture and a sin to eat.

Nights listening to plans Caleb made of things he would do,

places he would go with some of the older boys he loafed with, were the most exciting nights I spent. Places that he had mostly read about at Sourwood School and tacked on to. To me, his tales offered the best of two worlds: I could lay back and imagine a place and people exciting enough to bring a want big as Sourwood Mountain, and I never had to worry about his actually going off and leaving me alone since the tales were all talk and no go. Like the trip he had planned with Argus Rice to New Orleans. Riding down the Ohio to hook up with the Mississippi and on down to where people lived that ate crawdads mostly and girls went around dancing and looking for strangers. A place where if you got tired of eating crawdads you could ease off on oysters instead of the mussels too tough to eat here on the Sourwood River, pick off a pearl now and then, and come back upriver richer than Homer Spurlock. Or the place he had read about just a week this side of school letting out, where the men sat around on their rear ends, blowing through flutes and causing snakes to twine and dance. When I asked about a flute, he said it was like a piece of hollow-stemmed wood with one end daubed up and holes cut in it. You blew into one end and closed up the holes for notes. He talked about our making one: taking a piece of sumac and gouging the pulp out, closing one end and making holes, and practicing where Ma couldn't hear. Probably in the woods or along the rivers, wherever we could find a snake. Get good enough, he said, and you could blow and make a girl half-dressed dance a jig. I figured to stick with snakes.

Within a week, we found out more about the dog. And no wonder Caleb had looked on me with disgust the first day I had sized it up. I had missed what it really was by a country mile. I mean, it wasn't no ordinary hound dog, but a coach dog! Generva Spurlock had stopped by to pay Ma for some washing and ironing, and she had told Ma so. Snucked up, me and Caleb heard it all. How being a coach dog, she said, was nothing but high society! The uppities used them to trot along beside their big cars and horses, important-like, for show. Which didn't make sense to me. I mean, a dog silly enough to run beside a car or horse all day—it seemed like a sorry life to me. No varmint track to run, nothing to tree. Not even a stray cat. That Sourwood had never seen the likes was a sure thing. Caleb had already checked that out with Jobe Brummett, and there were two things about Jobe Brummett you could make mark on: 1) pulling a junk wagon around Sourwood twice a week, hauling garbage and throwaways from the homes of uppities only since commons rendered everything worthwhile down to nothing, Jobe knew more about the goings-on of society than anyone else, and 2) having had every dog in and about Sourwood chase his wagon one time or another, he had had a good look at every dog on the mountain. Generva owned the only coach dog there was. Whether the dog would end up chasing the junk wagon and Jobe too remained to be seen. Jobe hoped not; he owed a little money at the bank himself. What Generva left out concerning the high points of the society dog wouldn't have fit in Jobe's junk wagon.

After Generva left our house, Caleb shook his head and said, "Just as I figured."

"How's that?" I asked.

"I thought it might be a coach dog, though I never thought I'd live to see one," he answered.

Well, I figured Caleb was putting on. There was no reason why he should know about coach dogs even if he was ahead of me in school, reading and knowing worldly ways like he sometimes claimed he did.

"How come you know something like that?" I asked.

"Lots of ways," he answered. "But mostly from a book in the school library with words too big for you to cipher out."

That was the thing. Caleb never got stuck for an answer when it came to showing my ignorance, always laying off somewhere I had never been.

But, no matter. The society dog was here in Sourwood and he was living it up, causing rumors that stuck like burrs. One said the dog had a bed of its own, with a mattress stuffed with goose feathers that he ended up being allergic to, according to Doc Dinkle, who never doctored dogs but floating a little loan at the bank made an exception. Switching to duck down remedied the sleeping problem. Another said the dog ate liver mostly, its favorite food. The dog had all of its wants except for one thing: a horse or a fancy car to trot alongside.

Homer Spurlock took care of that, brought about, rumor was, to pacify Generva. With no place to keep a horse and, besides, Sourwood being mule country and a society dog too high up to trot alongside a mule, Homer turned to his Model A, the only car in town that ran. The car offered a chance to show the dog off and appease Generva.

It seemed to work. Of the mornings now, Homer Spurlock, his head high and important-like, drove up the dirt road to the bank with the spotted dog trotting along, heeled by the rear tires. Of the mornings now, Homer and the dog drew a crowd. And the dog did appear to be happy. At least for a few days. But the road being dirt was either dusty or muddy, and the big dog got to dropping farther and farther behind, clouded in dust or splattered with mud something terrible. Which made the trip harder, for Homer had to find a way to clean the dog off and then coax it to ride in the car home, which it wasn't inclined to do since its job was to trot and not ride, rumor was.

It was too exciting to miss. Boys staked out where they lived and rumored what passed through Generva's lips to pour on to poor Homer. It would have put a jaybird to shame.

And then one day the big dog got caught by a mud puddle and a backfire, and it dropped in its tracks. Doc Dinkle recommended bed rest and better roads. Since Sourwood was not willing to float a loan at the bank for road fixing, rumor was that the dog was being kept inside and humored to bedfast by Generva.

But being housed up didn't last long. The dog howled so mournful that Generva had to let it out. Once out, it shunned the town proper and headed for the riverbank where Caleb and I were spending the summer days. It was set to pester.

It ended up being pestering of the worst sort. I mean, it laid for us. Going after clothes Ma washed for Generva, we'd be ambushed. The dog would lay hidden on the porch and jump out at us with lips pulled above the sharpest teeth you ever saw on just one dog. It didn't have to bite even if it had had time. I mean, we climbed the tree in her yard faster than two squirrels, over and under trying to reach the highest limb. The clothes were scattered everywhere. Clothes either to be washed or gathered and washed again. We caught it from both Ma and Generva, and the big dog got off free.

Generva would come to our house fuming. Claiming as how Caleb and I had teased the dog and upset it so that it could not eat proper. She'd pucker her mouth and say, "You're just going to have to do something about your boys teasing my dog and climbing my tree. Breaking the limbs from a special tree that Homer had shipped all the way from Cincinnati to grow me a touch of home. The tree came from a seedling that grew in the governor's yard!"

After she was gone, Ma would quarrel because she feared losing Generva Spurlock as a washing customer. I'd tell Ma how it was that the big dog was mean and set to bite both Caleb and me. It never occurred to me that Caleb had never once struck a fault on the dog. Always, Ma would frown and say, "Let that be a lesson to you boys for pestering me so much for a dog of your own! Now you know the reason why I haven't given in. A dog is always trouble, always pestering by nature. Eats a lot, too. And we need all the money we can get just to make ends meet. Let it be a lesson to you both on my good judgment."

Life was miserable. The big dog had the jump and bluff on us, and we knew it. It came to the river every day to pester. Showing its teeth to us and daring us to do something about it. Our living along the river, it took to watching Ma hang clothes on the line to dry. It took to washed clothes like it took to liver. It'd grab them off the line and run to catch a river wind while the clothes, especially the sheets, quivered like ghost garments. Then it'd drop them off on the mud or sand, walking off with its tail still at high noon. We'd gather the clothes and Ma would wash again until her hands were red, all the time reminding us once again about the faults of a dog.

"You see the damage a dog can do?" she fussed. "Well, I just can't afford to lose Miss Spurlock as a customer, and so we'll just have to hang the clothes higher or hope the dog goes away."

Maybe it was seeing Ma's red hands that started Caleb thinking about doing something to stop the big dog stealing the clothes from the line—and helping us too along the way. That pleased me, for Caleb and I had gathered some driftwood along the river and added it to what had lodged in the forks of an old willow during high water and built us a treehouse. In between running two trotlines set and baited for channel cats, we lazied away the heat of day there, high enough to see the paddlewheels push tow up and down the rivers. The willow was old and slick and had lost its lower limbs to swift water during flood, and so we had made a makeshift ladder up it. Up high, we could see Ma's washings and hoped to coax the dog away.

The big dog delighted now in chasing me and Caleb up the tree and into the treehouse. It gnawed and growled at the rungs of the ladder, threatening to climb and snatch us out like birds out of a nest. When it wasn't gnawing, it walked around the treehouse with its tail at high noon. Stiff-legged and society-like, treeing us like two common opossums. Why, the river was no fun at all now. The big dog had stolen it all away. We had to sneak to fish and sneak to swim, with no loafing for fear of being caught somewhere along the bank. And the dog seemed to joy in it all. Stretched out in the warm sand to catch the morning or evening sun, or in the shade under our treehouse. He'd rise to his paws, bow in the middle from a stretch, and walk society-like and independent toward the river to drink from a cold spring that ran under the mountain and opened up near the river's edge. Life wasn't worth much with a society dog everywhere you looked or went.

It was on the day that the big dog almost got Caleb, ripped his britches leg halfway down while he struggled to get up the ladder, that he looked down from the treehouse and said, "We got to do something about that dog because of what it's doing to poor Ma."

He rubbed his leg, and I thought I'd tell him he might take a tongue-lashing from Ma with a rip like that in his britches but figured in the end he'd been through enough. I mean, that close to the dog's teeth! I just looked at poor Caleb sitting there with half a britches leg gone, his white skin striped by the sun that filtered through the cracks in the roof of the treehouse. Not being able to get out as much as usual and sprawl in the sun, his skin was as white as a skipjack for this time of year.

"That suits me!" I said. "Maybe we could figure a way to swing the dog from a willow!"

"And throw suspicion on Ma for doing away with a valuable dog like that?" Caleb said. "I mean, and waste all the time it's took me to coax it down here to the treehouse instead of stopping now at Ma's clothesline! Well, I ain't about to blow it all on a fool thing like that."

"What do you mean coaxing the dog down here to the treehouse!" I said. "It's been coming on its own, close enough to feel its breath, and you know it!"

"You really thinking it was coming on his own?" Caleb asked, but in a way that no matter my answer my ignorance would find me out.

"Yep," I answered.

"Well, that's just another reason why I lead and you follow," he said. "That dog comes here because I planned it that way. Just goes to show how little you know about dogs, especially society ones."

"I been following lately because you're older and faster than me," I said, "and that's all!"

"Had it planned since the dog stole Ma's first sheet," Caleb said.

Caleb stared me down, and I got to thinking that if I ever wanted to know what he had planned, if anything, I better join up. "Gosh, Caleb, that's something. I mean, poor Ma has suffered a lot."

"Well, I'm sorry about that," Caleb said. "Chasing me is one thing, but chasing the only brother I got is something else! And being slower, your britches and a thrashing from Ma could be a short time away. But the way I figure it, the dog's nabbed its last sheet!"

"Going to shoot it?" I asked, coaxing Caleb.

He drew up his mouth, and I knew that my ignorance had gone too far.

"Ain't you something to listen to!" he scolded. "Don't you know Pa would take the rap for that being he's the man of the house and owns the guns. With Pa looking out from behind bars, we'd all be shifting for ourselves, hungry and pining away. Besides, you don't shoot a society dog."

I set my mind not to be caught stupid again. Especially since I still knew nothing of Caleb's plan.

"I'm with you, Caleb," I said.

"That's better," Caleb answered. "Now you watch me close. I'm going to scratch my plans out on the floor of the treehouse just one time, up here where the dog can't see and you got to read it quick. I won't talk and chance being overheard."

Afraid I might miss something in Caleb's scratching, I said, "A dog can't read."

"We don't know," Caleb answered. "Common dog maybe not; society dog, who knows?"

Well, before I could say anything else Caleb was on all fours scribbling something terribly fast. Little bird-size scratches murky as a stirred mud puddle. I shook my head and looked down and saw that big dog with head high like it was trying to overhear. Or, maybe I was just shaky and the dog was listening to the scratching. I hoped Caleb couldn't see, afraid he might stop even if I couldn't read what he was scribbling.

But, no matter. Nearly as quick as he had started, Caleb rubbed his foot over what he had scratched, took a chew of life-everlasting weed, and looked independent-like. And he sure enough did look like something else, reared back chewing the weed as if it was real tobacco. It made me proud to be his brother, especially high up and being out of the reach of the dog for the moment. He was smart and then some. I mean, truth was, his plan might end up costing us both our britches, but Caleb had a way of making doom something to look forward to.

I watched Caleb now staring through the cracks in the floor, eyeing the big dog. His eyes worried me. They didn't look like the eyes on someone trying to do something in. They were more of a longing, a want. It scared me. I said, "Caleb, you'll get us both stripped down!"

The big dog had caught Caleb staring now. It showed his teeth and broke the silence over the river with its deep growling. Caleb paid no mind. He said, "That's just the way I see it. I mean, it didn't seem natural all along for a dog to go around treeing boys instead of cats. Why, it come to me that the dog needs us worse than we need it! That's the size of it."

"Looks to me like it's our britches legs it's needing," I answered.

Caleb didn't answer. I even doubted that he heard me. He was staring off over the river like he always did when he had a dream close up.

"You can tell by the way the dog's acting," Caleb said. "Boys need dogs, dogs need boys. It's not hard to figure now."

"I don't need a dog like that!" I answered. "What I want is a little dog what can snuck up in bed with me at nights, keeping ghosts away and the sorts. A belong-to-me dog that's got no truck with the likes of Generva Spurlock. One not too society for opossums and squirrels and got no loan at the bank on."

"And if I'm right in what I scratched out for you," Caleb said as if he had never heard what I said, "all we got to do is get together." He stared back between the boards. "Pretty, ain't it?"

"Longest teeth I ever saw on just one dog," I answered.

Well, we just lazied around in the treehouse scooting here and there to chance the rays of the sun that broke through, giving us something to do. Caleb glanced down now and then to check on the dog and throw a brag its way, which brought a growl. One thing was certain: the big dog wasn't taking to Caleb's sweet talk. It chewed on the lower rungs of the ladder, got mad because it couldn't climb, and then tore at the ground.

The only break we had coming up was that the big dog would leave at high noon to eat. That was its habit. Generva had told Ma that the dog was fussy that way. Expected liver, and on time. And so just this side of high noon, the big dog gave us a farewell growl and strutted off toward the top of the riverbank.

"Well, we got ourselves untreed," I said.

"That's right," Caleb answered. "And now we go to calculating. We know the dog will be back after it eats and takes a nap."

"Calculating!" I said. "What's that mean? We hardly got time to take a swim, let alone bait a line."

Caleb looked at me disgusted-like.

"If you was anywhere other than the low grades at Sourwood you'd know how to cipher my plan I scribbled out. You mean you didn't get any of it?"

"It all looked like little bird scratches to me," I said.

"Only chance you got now is to stick with me," Caleb said. "I ain't ever let you down before, have I?"

Scooting first down the ladder, I couldn't have counted the times. But I had little choice. Caleb was all I had.

Caleb's ciphering had strange ways. We couldn't go back to the treehouse after dinner because we had to gather washing around Sourwood for Ma. But we would sneak back to the river to make sure the dog showed at the treehouse after its noon nap. That was part of Caleb's plan. And so we did; hid among the sprouts and bugleweed and saw the spotted dog make its way over the bank. It reached the treehouse and seemed to sense right off that things weren't natural. It growled and showed its teeth. And then the dog stared off toward the treehouse and whined, mournful-like. And then searched around with its nose like it had lost something. Pitiful-like. It let out a wail.

"Just as I figured," Caleb said. "Lonesomer than lonesome. We'll be ready for that dog come morning!"

We spent the rest of the evening gathering clothes and helping Ma. On our way home Caleb stopped at Kelly's store and bought a nickel's worth of liver, which brought no suspicion since we often bought liver for trotline bait for catfish. Caleb asked Mr. Kelly to wrap the liver in wax paper, and he stuck it in his pocket. Once out of the store, he handed the liver to me and told me to hide it in the icebox until daylight. And then he told me he would see me this side of dark. That I was to tell Ma that he had picked up a job helping Mr. Kelly carrying produce set out for sale on the street to be stored inside overnight. And, if she was to ask, to tell her that Mr. Kelly only had work for one.

"Where you going?" I asked.

"Where I scribbled out," he answered. "Over to Jobe Brummett's to fish and turtle trade for some Jimsonweed seed to mix with the liver we take to the river to feed the big dog."

"Jimsonweed seed!" I said, loud enough to cause Caleb to look around to see if anyone was close enough for hearing.

"That's nightshade and poison. You'll kill that dog and we'll all be lawed!"

"Not kill the dog, silly," he said. "Mixed right to make it think what it ain't and do what it never thought it would. Acts the same as moonshine, mixed right."

Knowing that we had been taught to stay clear of things that belonged to the nightshade family, I said, "How you know that?"

"Well," he said, "I first picked the story up from Ringtail

Daulton, who picked it up from his pa, who traded a little moon-shine to Jobe for things he picked off now and then from the uppities. Ringtail says to me, 'How you figure Jobe Brummett has made it around mean dogs all these years without getting his legs gnawed down?' 'How's that?' I asked. 'Jimsonweed seed,' he says. 'Mixed right and fed right, it'll lay the hair down on a dog and friendly it next to pester. Time was, Jobe fought dogs from the homes of uppities until he thought of giving it up. He couldn't kick 'em off like commoners or yell until he was heard. It was get bit, lose business, or be lawed. That's when it come to him to try a little Jimsonweed seed. He knew it would put the wobbles to a man and make a woman want to snuggle up. Used right. He figured it was worth a try. Took a while to figure out the portion, but he did. Too much and a dog wanted to ride in his junk wagon and the uppities complained that he was leading their dogs astray. Finally he worked his way down to friendly, and they couldn't hardly wait for him to come for garbage. Hooked on it.'"

"What makes you think Jobe will do it?" I asked. "It ain't no common dog this time."

"You know how Jobe loves fish and turtle," Caleb said. "Throw in a couple of eels and Jobe will come to us next time." Caleb grinned. "Whooeee!" he said. "I can't wait. I mean, Ringtail says they go around lifting their legs trying to fly like birds and bumping into things trying to snuggle up with cockleburrs. Trying to get along with everything they touch, happy with the world in general and the sort."

"How long will the spell last?" I asked, thinking how nice it would be to swim and fish again without worry.

"It'll wear off," Caleb said. "But not before we've had a chance to make friends and truck around a little."

"You truck and I'll swim and fish," I answered.

It came to me that the liver mixed with Jimsonweed seed would be with me and Caleb in the treehouse. The big dog would be on the ground. I got worried that it might be me wrapped in plans I couldn't read that had to feed the dog. I never figured it would be dropped down on the sand. For if rumor was right, the society dog was picky and wasn't apt to eat on less than a clean plate. Some said it often ate from the table.

"Caleb," I said, "I been thinking. And the way it comes out, is I've changed my mind about dogs. I don't want one, for company or otherwise. All I want is the river, a joeboat, and a trotline."

If Caleb heard me he never let on. Sleep came slowly. But it came, and we were up and over to the river before morning had broken, liver and Jimsonweed seed in hand.

Once up in the treehouse, Caleb took an eyeglass he had made from a hollowed horseweed stalk and closed one eye and stared in the direction the society dog would be coming. He looked important-like peering through the weedglass like he was looking for a pirate ship instead of a dog. A spider ran down the chute and he knocked it out in the palm of his hand. He tried again.

We didn't have to wait long. I saw the big dog turning down the bank, told Caleb, and he fussed because he was supposed to have picked it off first, using the eyeglass and all. I swallowed.

"It's coming, Caleb," I said. "It's coming!"

"Don't I know that!" Caleb fussed. "I got the eyeglass, ain't I?"

Caleb pulled the liver from his pocket and laid it on the boards, with me thinking he should have brushed the boards before laying it there. And then he took some Jimsonweed seeds and measured, crushed, and mixed them with the liver.

Afraid that he would put more than the wobbles to the big dog even if he found a way to feed it, I said, "That do it?"

I waited for anything in our favor to be said.

"All part of what I know," Caleb said. "I aim to make that dog happy and then some. Fly like a bird or climb like a squirrel."

Scared, I said, "Not up in the treehouse, I hope!"

Caleb grinned. "Wouldn't matter even if it won't," he said. "It'll be friendly enough to make over."

Life wasn't worth much with a mean dog on the end of it. I

thought again of the scratching Caleb had made on the floor of the treehouse. I was afraid to ask what part included me and what included him. I worried that I was in the plan to do the first and maybe the last feeding. I was so wrapped up in doom that Caleb had to nudge me back. I swallowed.

"Caleb," I asked, shaky, "did I read right in the scratching that you would feed the dog and that I was to watch the bank to see that we didn't get caught?"

Caleb passed my words off like they were nothing, even though they seemed the most important ones of my life.

And then he all but snuffed me out. "We'll go according to plan. Which means that you go down the ladder first."

I swallowed again, almost starting to cry with thoughts of leaving this old world and all my friends including Caleb up to now.

"Tell Ma I said good-bye," I said.

But when I started down the ladder of doom, it looked as though providence had set on me like Ma once said it would if I built enough points toward it. If so, I figured I had just used them all up, maybe even getting a loan on if I lived long enough to pay back. I mean, the big dog had turned its back on me and was slowly walking off.

But before I had time to be grateful enough, Caleb spoiled it all. He puckered his lips and called the dog back. Stopped the big dog in its tracks. And me the only brother Caleb had!

The dog turned now and looked at me almost in disbelief that I was as ignorant as I was, climbing down to doom. Sent down as juicy as a plate of liver. It growled and showed its teeth, and I looked up and saw that Caleb's foot almost touched my nose. Thinking Caleb would call me back, I said, "What do you think, Caleb?"

"Just as I figured," he whispered. "The dog's hungry as a winter calf. See it open its mouth?"

I did and wished I hadn't. The big dog had teeth like a boar hog. Caleb slipped me a chunk of liver baited down, and it was slick and slimy to hold. The dog must have winded it. It threw its head into the air and snorted. At the liver, I hoped. For Caleb was punching me farther down the ladder with his foot.

Reaching the ground, I got me another favor. The dog just stood staring at me like the fool I was. Probably, I thought, stunned for the moment by my continued ignorance. It snorted the wind. And Caleb pulled down behind me. Glad for his company—any company other than the dog—I whispered, "What do you think, Caleb?"

"Just treat it like the society it is," Caleb whispered back. "Ease it the liver!"

Well, it made no sense. The big dog backed off instead of coming on. Which pleased me but not Caleb. Caleb clucked his lips and brought it back. He motioned for me to hold the liver high where the wind off the river would carry it smack in the dog's face. The dog licked its lips, which also showed its teeth.

"Stay in front and I'll check out the back to see if things are all right there," Caleb said.

"There's nothing back there but running room," I said. "The trouble's up front."

"Just follow the plan," Caleb scolded. Not knowing what the plan had been to begin with, I knew now that it was like usual— whatever he wanted it to be.

"The dog's showing his teeth at me!" I whispered.

"Hungry as a spring groundhog," Caleb said. "Just keep it society and edge closer. 'Pears like it likes you."

"Might you, too, if you would get around here," I said.

"Keep it society," Caleb coaxed.

Well, the way I saw it, a dog bite was a dog bite, society or common, with the hurt judged by the length of the teeth. Right now, high society appeared to have the edge.

"Caleb," I warned, "it's fixing to bite me!"

"Ain't you something to listen to," Caleb said, trying to shame me. "Maybe society don't go around biting commons like Ma and you."

The big dog showed its teeth, stared at the liver, and then backed off. Caleb worked his way up front where I was, maybe seeing that I was still alive.

"Come here, boy," he coaxed the big dog, clicking his lips.

The dog showed its teeth to Caleb and growled.

"What do you think now, Caleb?" I whispered, hoping he would see that the dog was not taking to sweet talk.

Caleb was shaking his head. "Shucks," he said, louder than I thought he ought. "Ain't that the doings. Far up in schooling as I am, I should have known that. I mean, all them books! Why, that dog ain't going to take to no common talk like we been using."

He sneered at the name "boy" he had used on the dog. "How common can you get? We got to put a title on that dog; something that's hitched up to society in the worst sort."

"What about Clovie?" I asked, thinking of the name of one of the uppities in town.

"Shhhhhhhh!" Caleb whispered. "You'll insult that dog beyond where we can get above. We got to be careful. One more mistake might do us in."

Caleb rubbed his head, thinking. I tried to eye the ladder without moving my head and figure which leg I wanted to give away if I didn't make it all the way. I saw Caleb smile.

"Come here, Your Maharaja!" he said, coaxing me to hold out the liver for a take.

Seeing the big dog still staring, I whispered, "What sort of name is that to tack on a dog?"

"Royalty," Caleb whispered. "The highest sort. That's what they call the kings in the sand country we studied about at Sourwood School. You can't get no higher than that. I told you and Ma about it."

Trying to remember, I asked, "How far did you say it was?"

"Well, you can't get there in a joeboat," he answered.

Remembering now, I thought of how it had made no sense back then and made less now with a big dog staring on the end of it. A land far off without enough water to swim in and only figs to eat. Ma hadn't taken too lightly to it either. Especially the part where the women all went around in tiny skirts exposing themselves something awful. She figured the law ought to have done something about that and here too if that was what they were teaching down at Sourwood. Girls dancing around to flutes along with snakes, both low-bellied in her mind.

But, Caleb had it figured this way: the big dog being here on sand made the name proper. And it did appear like Caleb might have been right. I mean, a change had come over the dog. Every time Caleb called out the highbrow name, the dog would perk up its ears. Which bothered me since it showed my ignorance. I mean, a dog knowing a foreign language like that instead of me. It beat all!

Caleb clicked his lips and highbrowed the big dog right up to biting distance. It reached out to take the liver and then backed off. Stopped in its tracks and closed its jaws, which I thought was comforting to me. Things looked a little better. Maybe the dog wasn't smart enough to know it was being called royalty. Maybe it didn't know a foreign language ahead of me. I thought it struck the dog with a little common like me.

"What do you think, Caleb?" I whispered.

But Caleb paid me no mind. He went about shaking his head in disgust about something, ungrateful, I thought, for not being bit by now.

"Something up?" I asked.

"No wonder we ain't getting nowhere!" Caleb said, shaking his head and with a silly grin on his face. "Why that dog's a Maharanee! I just now took notice." Stuck with ignorance again, I whispered, "Well, good gosh. Wouldn't you know. We better get back up in the treehouse then."

"Ain't you something to listen to?" Caleb fussed in pure disgust. "It don't have nothing to do with leaving! It just means that the dog's a she instead of a he! A squatter instead of a riser. I don't know why I never noticed that before!"

But I had. The problem was on the front end instead of the rear as far as I was concerned.

"Yep, she is a Maharanee, a queen what's done away with the king and is up and giving the orders." Caleb looked down at the spotted dog. "Open your mouth and take the liver, Your Maharanee, and excuse my little brother's ignorance!"

The big dog winded the liver again and looked at Caleb. She opened her mouth slowly.

"Ease the liver now," Caleb said. "Your favorite, and fit for a queen."

It beat all! I mean, the Maharanee swallowed the liver in one gulp, which Ma would have scolded me for doing. For some reason, I thought society would eat like a bird, picky and in little bites, and as silent as a shooting star.

Well, the big dog sat down on its haunches, and me and Caleb waited and watched. Waited for little changes that ought to be taking place. It didn't take long. The first sign was that she sort of floated to her feet and stood staring out over the river. Then she walked slowly toward it, swinging her legs in and out like the oars of a joeboat. And Caleb, with more nerve than I thought he ought to have, walked off to the river with her. Caleb looked back at me like the dog was following him instead of him her.

At the edge of the river, she stopped for a moment and then stepped in as if she expected the surface to hold her. It didn't, and she got wet good and proper before stepping back to shake water all over Caleb. And then she licked his hand. Caleb, wet as a chicken caught in the rain, smiled silly-like and said, "Ain't that something? She followed me to the river like she was trotting beside a horse!"

While it had looked the opposite to me, seeing Caleb as happy as he was, I wasn't about to say different. I had never seen him so happy, like he had all his wants in his pocket.

The big dog, glassy-eyed now, just stood and looked off like it was searching for nothing that you could speak of. Caleb reached down and patted her on the head. She wagged her tail like she had set to make amends for all the trouble she had caused.

"I got me a dog now," Caleb said. "A society dog!"

"How long will that stuff last?" I asked, fearing for the both of us when the Jimsonweed wore off.

Caleb didn't answer. He was making over the dog now something awful, and she was acting like they had always been. I figured when she got her wobbles straightened out and her eyes fixed, she would come snapping. While I hated the thought, it did cross my mind that Caleb, being so close, would be the first to go. With luck, I could make the treehouse.

"We'll spend some time together along the river," Caleb said. "Being with me awhile ought to do it."

Poor Caleb. I wished it had turned out that way. But the big dog finally set her eyes toward the top of the bank. And all the coaxing Caleb could muster up wouldn't stop her. She turned up the bank, stopping here and there like she was trying to fly or something. She must have traveled a hundred yards to make twenty feet, circling and all. Finally she was gone from sight.

Hoping to ease some of the pain from Caleb, I said, "Want to go swimming?"

Caleb looked so downcast. "I don't feel like it," he said, staring off the way the big dog had gone.

Caleb moped around the rest of the day. He wouldn't swim, fish, or traipse the banks to see what the current had brought downriver worth keeping. I mentioned running a new trotline, but Caleb turned that down. He moped right into bedtime, and Ma never had to quarrel at us for talking in bed.

We were up early and on our way back to the treehouse. We waited a while but the big dog didn't show. Caleb seemed to rule the river out. All he wanted to do was hang around the treehouse in case the dog showed. We loafed until noon and then went home to help Ma. Ma sensed something. "I haven't seen that big dog around my clothesline this morning to pester. I just might hang out some sheets."

She saw that what she said had not set right with Caleb. Ma was like that, able to sense without being told when it came to me and Caleb. She put her hands on her hips and stared at him.

Well, Caleb moped for the better part of three days, until we got some word of the big dog. Generva Spurlock came by and told Ma she would have a wash ready near the end of the week and that me and Caleb could pick it up on Friday, watching her grass and flowers while we did so. Ma mentioned that she hadn't seen the big dog lately. Me and Caleb sneaked close to listen.

Generva Spurlock told Ma that she had never witnessed the likes of what had happened. The dog had come up from the river paddling sideways with her feet and then jumped off the porch like she was trying to fly. She tried to make amends to everything she bumped into, like she owed it an apology of sorts. Friendly— up until Generva got afraid it might follow a stranger off. Well, finally she had had to call Doc Dinkle. He wasn't long coming.

"If I didn't know better, I'd say this dog was drunk," he said. And seeing the look on Generva's face, he added, "but, fact is I do know better. This dog has come down with a rare virus, a virus for some unknown reason only picks on important dogs what are registered and the sort. In all my years of doctoring, I've never known the virus to pick on a common dog."

But the word *drunk* had stuck with Generva, and she had to shake it. She drew up her mouth to show Ma her rage. "'Doc Dinkle,' I said. 'You watch your tongue! I'm not about to pay a doctor's fee to someone that says my dog is a common drunk. I'll have you know that dog is registered!'"

And so it was. Generva was keeping the big dog penned up inside on duck down.

"It's a strange thing," she told Ma. "She won't eat her liver and seldom sleeps. Just goes to the window and stares out toward the river where she probably picked up the virus in the first place. Acts like she wants to risk it again, a drawing power there of sorts."

Well, that caused Caleb to mope even more. Later that evening

Ma said to us, "You know, I been doing some thinking. You boys have been good to work and help me. Jobe Brummett stopped by while you were at the river the other day and mentioned that he had some pups on his place out of the big one-eared cur of his, but a fairer-than-middlin' rat dog. Maybe you boys have earned one to traipse with you. But it stays outside, you know."

It pleased me but did nothing for Caleb. Ma saw so and said, "Something wrong, Caleb? The dog comes for two or it don't come at all."

"I don't want a dog, Ma," Caleb answered.

Ma frowned. "Well, you think about it," she said.

Later that night Ma caught Caleb off moping and said, "Caleb, it's natural to want something you can't have. I always wanted a washer but never had money to buy one. Now, the big dog belongs to someone else and it never would have worked out anyway. Registered society dogs are for people like Generva Spurlock mostly and common dogs like the ones Jobe Brummett has are for people like us, to make out of them what we can. We don't have money for liver and hardly have enough scraps. Better to choose a pup from Jobe Brummett and teach it to leave my sheets alone."

"But, Ma," Caleb said.

"Think about what I said," she said. "Do it before I change my mind."

On Friday, me and Caleb went over to Generva Spurlock's house to gather clothes. And that's when it happened. I mean, when the door was open, the big dog got wind of Caleb. I thought it would wag its tail off. She whined until Generva took to scolding. It was pitiful. And Caleb stood, helpless to throw his arms around the dog.

We got the clothes, and the big dog tried to follow. But Generva scolded and locked her up. I couldn't figure it out. The big dog making a fuss over Caleb without one Jimsonweed seed in her.

"Caleb," I said, "I do believe that dog has took a liking to you something awful."

"All she ever needed was for me to pet her," Caleb said. "To know that I was her friend. I just had to get close once for her to know."

Seeing the big dog again had made it worse. I wished we had never picked up the clothes, and I told Ma so.

"He'll live through it," Ma said. "Once he gets a pup from Jobe and rubs his hands over it, the change will come."

I hoped Ma was right and we could end up getting a pup from Jobe. Life was hardly worth living with Caleb moping around like he was.

That night at supper, someone knocked on our door and Ma went to answer. She opened the door, and we held our breath seeing Generva Spurlock standing there. It hit me that she had come to complain about something me and Caleb had done, but I couldn't think of a thing we had. I heard Caleb drop his fork. Ma invited her in.

"No," she said, "I haven't time. I came to tell you how strange it was that my dog was sick and how it was that not even Doc Dinkle had a cure. And yet today, when your boys came, she showed signs of healing right off. I got to thinking. With me being gone so much during the days, society club meetings, flower shows, and the likes. And the dog being left alone. And . . . well . . . what I'm trying to say is that, truth be, a dog is made for boys, not for an old woman too set in her ways. Boys and dogs go natural together, you know."

"How well I know," Ma answered.

"Well," Generva said, "I dropped by to see if your boys would let her come to the river some to be with them. Take away the loneliness."

"There would be the matter of sheets," Ma said.

"She could be broke from that," Generva said.

"Then I think it would be fine," Ma said.

"I'll turn her loose in the morning," Generva said. "I'll let the boys get back to their eating."

"I think they just finished a moment ago," Ma said.

Caleb said that the night would never end, but I fell asleep and it did. At daybreak, we were sitting in the treehouse watching the high bank. Caleb was so happy that he gave me the eyeglass this time and I used it. Even though I saw better without it, I felt more important-like.

And then a circle of white and black spotted fur filled the glass and Caleb knocked the glass out of my hand to reach the ladder. Still not sure what the big dog would do, I held back and watched. Caleb pulled a small piece of liver from a wrapper and gave it to the dog. She swallowed it and licked at his hand.

"There will be more later on, Your Maharanee," Caleb said.

The big dog glanced at me but did not show its teeth. I took a chance and stepped down the ladder. Caleb was rubbing the big dog on the head and speaking soft words to her.

"What do you think, Caleb?" I asked.

"I'm ready to set trotlines and swim," he said.

And we walked off toward the river where we had tied the joeboat. The big dog trotted along beside Caleb like a society dog would do. It beat all.

On our way upriver, Caleb stopped oaring to stare at a paddlewheel pushing tow against a current. Some men standing on deck were staring off at us, and I figured they were making over the big dog riding the back seat. They waved and we both waved back. I felt good, being part of a big society dog, a little yondside of common for the first time in my life.

"Caleb," I said. "That's something having a coach dog riding in a joeboat with you."

"You ain't seen nothing yet," Caleb said, pulling on the oars. "Wait until she runs alongside the boat."

I figured Caleb was happy and kidding. But with Caleb, there was never any sure way of knowing.

On Joe
Carter's Mule

It all started with Mose Alley. I mean the way it happened with Joe Carter's mule. Not for what Mose could remember, but for what he couldn't. The way it ought to be for the making of a good rumor: enough room left on the end for add-ons.

Mose held two titles in Sourwood: he was the town drunk, but also the finest butcher ever to work on the mountain. From slaughtering to special cuts. Slaughtering being, according to Caleb, the reason Mose had turned and stayed to drink. Caleb said all butchers generally ended up this way because of the undertakerish sort of life they had to live. One slaughtering and the other waiting, both were dressing out a corpse but for a different ending.

Whenever Mose wasn't butchering, he was either leaned up against the side of an old building in town for support while he glared out at passersby, squinting to recognize them, or over on the river trying to coax boys to listen to what he had to be drunk enough to do, stories that would raise the hair on your head and jump out at you nights later whenever you stayed on the river to fish. He never saw singles, but three or four of whatever he looked at. In town passersby were as thin as hen's teeth, yet Mose claimed, according to the numbers he saw, the town was getting too crowded to find room to hug up to a building anymore. On the river, when he forked you over with a finger, there were always three or four of you, and you had to answer to three or four names to coax out a story that he started, something mournful that was always too sad to listen to but too exciting to let go of.

Old-timers swore by him, claiming that he was king of the mountain when it came to sizing up a carcass and making the right cuts. He knew grass-fed from grain-fed and could slice the cut to fit the condition of your teeth. The price he set meant nothing, being as he never did the selling.

Mose wore the same clothes all the time, including a pair of hobnailed boots that sparked rocks to tell of his coming and left holes in the ground to tell of his going. His clothing was faded out and splotched with red—everyone knew what from, especially boys, but each had different stories to tell, spookiness and hand-holding being the only thing the stories had in common. He smelled enough to draw flies and never washed, even at the river, claiming water broke him out in hives.

Mose worked for Lyle Martin, who owned and operated the Sourwood slaughterhouse and meat market. Lyle operated out of a large one-story building, the store in front and the slaughterhouse tacked on the back. And while he sold other produce that came off the mountain in season, like berries, herbs, and the sort, meat was his specialty. Known far outside the limits of Sourwood, people came from as far away as West Virginia and Ohio, crossing the Sourwood and Ohio Rivers to get there.

Lyle was short and thin and had a nightshadish color about him, which you sort of expected, his being owner of the slaughterhouse and all. But he was generally friendly and would take time to slice off a nickel's worth of liver whenever you wanted some-

thing that would stay on a hook and take a catfish or turtle, especially liver with the skin left on to thread a hook through. On days
when chickens were slaughtered, he would trade guts for berries,
guts that I would take to the river to spoil in the sun and ripen for
trotlining. He would stand at the front of the store with his hands
on his hips, laughing while he watched the flies boil after me like
clouds on my way down to the river. I figured his laughing was
small payment for the fish and turtles I could take back and sell to
him. I also caught carp fish that no one in town would eat—carp
being considered a gutter fish, living on blood dumped into the
river by the slaughterhouse and funeral home—and sold them back
to him dressed out as catfish, without anyone knowing. A secret I
was afraid to tell Caleb, because Caleb said Lyle was always close
to death and funeral-like.

All in all, Lyle got along with most people in and around
Sourwood except for Joe Carter. Joe was the only competition Lyle
had, not in meat but in all other things he sold that could come off
the mountain—garden produce, berries, nuts, herbs, and the sort.
There was a running battle between the two of them, almost a
feud. Each underselling the other, making it a loss for both. Lyle
claimed Joe could undersell being as he had no overhead, and Joe
claimed the opposite being as mountain produce was all he had
while Lyle had meat to make up. But Caleb said the reason was
deeper than that, that each was set to outsmart the other.

Joe Carter was a ribly sort of man, much older than Lyle,
bird-breasted and with a hump on his back. Living over on Blaine,
he came to Sourwood on Saturdays to buy provisions and peddle
what he had gathered off the mountain. He always rode in on his
grey-slated mule, Rachel, a mule that was eyed two ways: either
the mule and the old man had grown to each other, or they had
been together long enough for the mule to become as ornery as Joe
was. The mule was so old that this would probably be her last year
coming to town. He'd always tie the mule off to a tree inside the
town limits to keep her from picking along the streets while he

bought and peddled. Afterwards, Joe always dropped over to the riverfront saloons to buy a little-boy bottle to sip on for his rheumatism on the way back to Blaine. No matter his condition, Rachel knew the way home and she'd get him there.

By the time I had come to know Joe Carter, he was on the low end of the feud with Lyle Martin. Where once men along the mountain would have been quick to bet on the outcome either way, bets on Joe were now hard to come by, and at best demanded odds as high as bird-fly. But Caleb said he had heard tell that the oldest on the mountain warned about betting against the old man. It was a fight between mountain-smart and town-raised. Mountain-smart they claimed Joe to be, cunning as a fox and known to sull like an opossum to get close to the throat. But there were more doubters than believers, especially since it was a town fight, and Lyle had the advantage of being in town all the time, with Joe coming in once a week.

Good words were becoming harder to find around Sourwood on Joe and especially on Rachel. People bought from him now with caution. Rumor was that berries he sold could be topped with dewberries large as bird eggs but bottomed with sunberries small as fox grapes. He had to carry two buckets now, one full of berries, and one empty to be used for pouring the one into the other so that buyers could be sure of what they bought. With rumors that a wild duck could favor a coot bird, buyers demanded the head be left on. Eggs could be fresh or taken from a hen after a week's setting along the mountain. And specks in his honey were said to be the remains of dead bees, proving that he had smoked the hives too hard or robbed them of their winter keep. Joe sold for less and tried to make do.

Rachel fared no better around Sourwood now than Joe. Tolerance for her was thin. The Younger Women's Society in Sourwood turned on her in the worst way. Where once she had caught some of the blame for eating flowers planted by them to show off the town to strangers who seldom came, now she caught it all, the club members claiming she broke her tie-rope and roamed. Loss to rabbits, dry weather, and the sort was ruled out.

Never staying in one place, Rachel was bad to traipse. Each Saturday soon after Joe had tied her off, she'd slip the tie and spend most of the day nibbling at anything growing along the street in town. She did nibble her share of flowers set by the Younger Women's Society and knock down lines of washed clothes hung low along the river to dry. She was mule-smart and then some, having lived long enough along the mountain to soak up all there was to know about mischief from both Joe and the mountain. Especially Joe. She knew when it was time for him to go back to Blaine, and she was always there ahead of him, her head bowed from innocence, swishing flies with her tail like she had been there as long as the mountain itself. A gospel mule whose next trip would be to the Pearly Gates.

After a few sips from the little-boy bottle, Joe never knew whether she had slipped the tie or not. As little as he was, he got rowdy at times after he'd had a few drinks, and boys were afraid to tell him about the mule, coaxed on by members of the Younger Women's Society to do so. Back to the mountain she'd go, with Joe riding full-saddle, side-saddle, back-saddle, or over her back like a sack of feed.

It was only a matter of time, Caleb said, until the women's club, coaxed now by Lyle's wife, fussed so much that Joe finally had to tie the mule off just this side of the town limits where Sourwood had no jurisdiction. He tied her off in a field beside the slaughterhouse with enough grass to pay to lengthen the rope so she could graze while he was in town. And although he wasn't a great distance from where he had left the mule in the first place, it was the principle of it, Joe had told Caleb. When I asked what that meant, Caleb said the answer was beyond the grade I was in at school. So I let it go at that, like I did so many other things he gave me no answer for.

When it came to Joe, Caleb also said it was only a matter of time. Even now, with what he brought to sell in Sourwood hardly worth the gathering, and the mule catching the blame for eating everything that grew green, he'd probably give it all up before the year was out. To make matters worse, the Younger Women's Society worked to bar all mules entering from beyond the town limits. Knowing that Lyle had an interest in the matter and was a vote, they sought his help and had no trouble passing the new law. Lyle had gone there with intentions of driving the last nail in Joe's coffin.

Joe fought back the best he could even without being able to vote, living outside the town limits. He spread rumors of how it was not Rachel nibbling the flowers and sorts, but animals brought in for slaughter by Lyle, kept over and getting loose to run the town at nights until being caught before daylight and brought back. How Lyle was too stingy to feed last meals. And how making a hog mad before dressing it out made the meat strong. But, you couldn't get a bet on Joe winning no matter the odds. Word was that Council had called a meeting to end the matter once and for all, top-heavy for Lyle, who offered them special discounts. We all waited.

On Saturday, Joe rode the old mule to the field outside the city limits and tied her off before he walked into town. The weather was a mixture of light rain and snow. Caleb and some of the older boys had seen him while on their way to the river to see if the ducks had begun to circle the West Virginia point, searching for food in the willow seedlings that grew several feet out in the shallow water. They had laughed and made brags as how Rachel would slip the rope and make her way behind Joe without his seeing.

The weather turned to a snow, and Joe did not stay in town as long as usual. Neither did Caleb and the others, having seen no ducks turning the point. The boys were at the field when they saw Joe flailing his arms and screaming for his mule, who was nowhere in sight. Joe swayed from side to side like he was searching the snow for mule tracks. He saw the boys and offered to pay anyone who would help him look for his mule. He picked Arlis Perkins, who saw ghosts in his backyard, would wail out at anything, and could spread a rumor before you had finished what you wanted him to say, but adding to it even worse than you had intended. At tracking, he was the worst of the lot, the last dog in the pack.

Caleb said it suited all that Arlie was chosen to look for the mule, knowing that Joe wasn't much to pay on a promise and wondering whether it was even him that spoke or the little-boy bottle. The weather was getting cold, and Joe having returned to the field a little early, they were all sure the old mule would probably beat the two of them back to the field. But, too curious to give it up at that, the boys picked sentries among them to stake out the town until the mule was spotted coming back.

The way it turned out, Joe, with Arlie following behind, caught what he took to be the mule's tracks and worked them like a hound, unraveling them out of the snow as he walked, bent low to the ground. Arlie backed him up even though he wouldn't have known a mule's track from a bird-wallow. The tracks led in the direction of the slaughterhouse.

Stopping only once to rest because Joe had become worried about something bad that had happened up front, Arlie stepped up his pace, squinting now from side to side, uneasy with Joe's voice. Reaching the back side of the building, Joe thought he saw where Rachel had stopped to nibble on a bale of hay for feeding holdovers awaiting slaughter. And then he lost her tracks among those of other animals. Tired and wet, he dropped down on the hay and stared off. Finally, hearing Mose inside the slaughterhouse, he looked inside.

And then Arlie heard Joe's wail and followed his point. Inside the slaughterhouse he saw Mose working over a large corpse stretched out on a bed of boards. Above it hung a grey-mottled hide that, in the shadows, could have been taken for anything but did have Rachel's color. It looked bigger than natural, and Mose, swaying from side to side and probably seeing three or four of whatever it was, was humming a song that made no sense. And then Joe said it: "My mule! Lyle has slaughtered old Rachel!"

That's all it took. Arlie could handle the rest, and did. Slipping and falling, he ran through town spreading word that Lyle had had Mose slaughter Rachel like a common steer. Mauled her beyond recognition!

Before the snow had covered Arlie's tracks, people were leaning over fences asking neighbors if they had heard about Joe Carter's poor old mule, Rachel. They braved the snow to stop passersby and gather further word; anything they could build to.

"Dreadful!" they said. "And in front of the eyes of a child! Passed here almost scared out of his mind!"

Someone said Joe was humped up to a tree staring off sad and mournful, hardly breathing. Probably in shock. Like he had lost his next of kin. They allowed as how someone ought to check on him, and several did. Each brought back tales that rent the heartstrings too short to tie. What could they say? What could you say at a time like this? An old man and his trusted mule. One snapped away from life in the blink of an eye. Cut short by a common drunk on orders from Lyle Martin! A poor beast of burden the likes of which had cleared the mountain country for crops and served man well. Surely, she had deserved better than a hammer and a butcher knife. People walked by Joe now, their heads lowered like flags, like they were viewing a coffin. Joe looked the part. I told Caleb so when we took our turn to pay respects while he was still in town. His was a favorable crowd, all in all, with most appreciating Joe sitting there mourning for something that would never return. She would be missed in Sourwood. Poor Rachel, struck down in old age still trying to help Joe make a living when things ought to have eased up, and on her last year coming to town, old and broke-down.

It was so sad that I told Caleb how bad I would miss her too, and instead of fussing at me over a mule that was changeable like Joe, and bad to bite if you got too close, he told me he would, too.

As bad as the day had been, what followed made a pauper of it. In less than a week you couldn't have gotten a bet on Lyle to win the feud betwixt him and Joe! Not only had he allowed Mose to snuff out the mule in her golden years, but—with a little help from Joe, in mourning and coming to town more often, trying to retrieve the remains for burial—Lyle had tried to buy her carcass. Odds favored the mule and the old man of the mountain.

Rumors were thicker than the ducks that had come now to the West Virginia point to feed. One had it that Lyle had gone to Blaine to try to strike some settlement with Joe. To make amends. People shook their heads. They searched Mose out for gossip. Catching Mose off and out of sight of the store, they tried priming him every way they knew how. All he could say was that whatever it was he had slaughtered, there were three of them.

It got worse. Jim Maynard remembered buying a wild rabbit from Lyle's store a week or so earlier and thought it was funny at the time that the rabbit had been dressed out, since Lyle generally hung them on hooks outside his store with the fur on. Stranger still, cutting it up to fry, he had noticed a few strands of yellow hair on the carcass: the same color as on the cat he had lost a few days before! A good mouser! Caged and brought in by Lyle, who had always been greedy enough to lift the penny from a dead man's eye. Mose had never known the difference.

Joining Caleb and the others now, I added to, trying to out-rumor the lot of them, which was hard. I mean, by this time Lyle had already caught the blame for every dog, cat, or other four-legged varmint that had disappeared around Sourwood! Even chickens now that had flown the coop or been lifted out by a fox. If there was a fox left. Add-to's were hard to come up with.

We talked along the river about how much hamburger you could grind off a big mule, time healing our talk about her some like time will on things passed on. Though Arlie still cried and hung close enough to pester, afraid. We mocked, passing one another on the way to rebait a handline:

"How you feeling today, Chet?"

And Chet would grab his belly and groan. "Poorly and awful sad." And then instead of belching, he'd bray.

"How come poorly?" someone would ask.

"Et something at Lyle Martin's," he'd answer.

"How come sad?"

"I can't find old Shep," he'd answer.

With his business on the rocks, Lyle set about harder to make amends. First off, he agreed to build another slaughterhouse farther from town, something the Younger Women's Society had been trying to get him to do forever because of Mose and the mournful bawl of animals that scared little children in town. It was rumored that he would turn the old building over to the town to be used for club meetings and the sort, with a pretty place for flowers in front. Rumor was also that he had at last struck a deal with Joe Carter, the agreement allowing Joe to bring his produce off the mountain to be sold at a fair price at the new store, with Lyle offering nothing in competition to it. They talked about what a fine Christian man Lyle could be. If he made amends and repented for his misdeeds, which included Mose.

Lyle tried to sober Mose up. Bought him a new suit to wear, but Mose only put it away, claiming already three suits to be buried in when and if his time come. Old mountain men who had favored Joe collected on their bets, bragging of his mountain-raising and the lessons to be learned from it.

But all in all, I thought, it was still a sad time. Everything had worked out for everyone except the mule. She had paid the price for it all, not even getting a decent burial. I thought of her now on every trip I made along the mountain. Once I saw her above Joe's cabin and had watched her struggle to pull a tuft of grass to eat, teeth too worn for a grass-hold. I shouldn't have let her struggle, even if she was bad to bite and known to kick.

I mourned right up to the day I was up behind Joe's cabin and, staring down, saw the old mule there. Her head was sticking out of the barn door and her rear end was still inside. She was looking around like she was trying to see if she was alone, if all around was clear. First off, I wondered if I was seeing a mule-ghost in broad daylight! And then I saw her bend to pull at a tuft of grass and knew better.

With a mind full of mule, I never heard Joe coming up behind me. I nearly jumped out of my britches. He had been silent as daybreak. Glancing at the mule, I saw that she had seen me. She ducked her head back inside the barn, as if she had been taught to. I felt Joe nudge me and turned to face him.

"You see a mule, boy?" he asked, pushing a sawbuck toward me.

And for greed, all I saw was the sawbuck. A chance maybe for more money than I had ever owned in one piece.

He added, "If you didn't, the sawbuck's yours!"

I stared toward the barn. It had been Rachel all right. Alive and well and smart enough to hide out. And I realized now that the way it had been on that fateful day was that Joe had planned it all. That he had doubled back to bring the mule home and then returned without her. Mountain-smart, cunning.

And then for some reason, I thought of Caleb. How it was he always fussed at me for not doing the right thing but for following the truth of it. Why wasn't I more like him on things of this sort? This day, I decided, I would be. No matter the cost. Doing exactly what I knew Caleb would do, I reached out and took the sawbuck.

"If you ever do," Joe added as I turned to go, "I'll come looking!"

I left him and the mule there, wondering as I did so which of what I had would keep the longest, the sawbuck or the secret!

The Cornstalk
Fiddle

When Nathan's grandmother died, his father coaxed his grandfather into moving into the hewed-log cabin behind their farmhouse. It stood close enough to be seen but far enough for voices not to be overheard. And that was important. For the old man was furiously independent. Especially now when his life had become too lonely and the winters had grown too long. He needed to be watched without knowing it.

They helped move him in early spring, and he chose to bring his small yellow Jersey cow and mule, Sam—a cow that his hands were too arthritic to milk and a mule a quarter century old that he had lost the desire to work.

Before the move, Nathan had gone to his grandfather's house to learn how to milk and to see that Sam had feed. When the animals were brought to the cabin, Nathan fixed a place in a shed for the cow and mule and fenced off a short pasture for them to graze in until they got accustomed to their new home.

Until near the end of winter his grandfather tried to keep

house alone, but with his heart not in it, he failed miserably but did not complain. He lived in the past, in a mixture of memory and forgetfulness. Being married for more than seventy years built many memories, but Nathan's father said forgetfulness often came with age.

Bringing the cow and mule to their new home, a walking distance away, Nathan's grandfather had cautioned him to dodge briars along the way that might scratch the Jersey's udders and make her too sensitive to milk. He cautioned that a mule not working needed only hay but no grain.

Falling back occasionally and out of hearing, Nathan's father spoke of Nathan's grandfather having a body that could no longer do what his mind wanted, although the will to do was probably even greater now than in his younger years, his fear of becoming a burden greater than ever. Often he had heard his father say that idleness was the devil's handmaiden, and that hands and minds were meant to be busy. He worried that his father alluded to his childhood too often now and expected age as the cause. He should not be left alone more than necessary. And since his work as a coal mine inspector kept him away weekdays as well as weekends at times, Nathan was to watch over him without being seen to watch over except for want of company. It was a tall order but one that Nathan looked forward to. For his grandfather was judged, not only by his mother and father but also by others, to be one of the smartest men ever to live on Sourwood Mountain.

Even now, when his grandfather left things untold either from loss of memory or interest, there was still so much to be learned. Nathan loved the mountain almost as much as he loved his grandfather. That others believed in the old man's mountain knowledge also was not long in being shown. After he had moved into the cabin in the back of the house, people who had long known or heard of his mountain magic began to trickle in. His knowledge of herb cures was unmatched. Add to his being a seventh son and possessing powers to cure thrush in children by blowing down their throats and to stop bleeding by the laying on of his hands. When Nathan had asked his mother about this once, she had said that believing he could do so was the first step to healing.

Some came to find a start of heirloom seed generations old that he kept and believed in. From eight-row corn to redheart tomatoes. Seed that held flavor and the proven ability to survive on the mountain. He feared the day might come when pure seed might be gone from the mountain forever. And so he cautioned them to save some back to pass on. He was said to be able to witch water from a rock, using a fork from either a peach tree or a wild plum, which he told Nathan once that he preferred of the two. But so old now, his back arthritic and bowed, he no longer practiced it.

Nathan's father and mother never encouraged people's coming, especially his father. It had been too soon after Nathan's grandmother's death, and visitors' talk was often too remindful of her. Of the ones who came, the children seemed to bother the old man the most. They cried and seemed to be more afraid of him than before, afraid now to come to his lap. His flock of white hair unkempt and the faded overalls down in the front from the bow of his back, he went unshaven for days on end and took little care of himself; at times he would forget and holler for Nathan's grandmother to come help him. His face was heavily wrinkled and his eyes sunken, dark and shadowed. For the older who came, it never mattered; for the younger it did. Nathan heard the younger say how shriveled up he had become.

Nathan's father spoke of stopping their coming altogether. But, then, watching his father sitting alone on the porch staring into nothing over the mountain, he changed his mind. At least for the present. For their coming gave the old man something to do, a feeling of being needed. A day-to-day forbearance; time passing in hopes of healing the loneliness inside him, making his life bearable.

Of the days now, after their trips to the cemetery where his grandmother was buried, Nathan sat with his grandfather on the cabin porch watching the old man cheat the sun with a straw hat. They were always there before the morning had broken to watch the sun come over the top of the mountain. He listened to his grandfather talk of the past mostly, his voice at times trailing off into a whisper. But often, like sun through a cloud, his sadness turned into a smile, and he would remind Nathan that a smile was to be judged by how long it lasted after it had been created.

He told stories going back further than others on the mountain had ever lived to go. He was considered the oldest on the mountain left, his tales and happenings exciting enough to steal Nathan's breath away. Some of them seemed unbelievable, taller than the mountain itself, with no way to sort truth from fiction. Mixed in was his grandfather's forgetfulness, which often left a tale unfinished and Nathan wanting. Many of these he later told to his mother hoping that she might have heard them before and remembered the ending. She seldom if ever did, but she cautioned Nathan that it was important his grandfather never be told of his forgetfulness. Important to show no signs of an unfinished tale, but to learn to make up his own endings. As for separating truth from fiction, what difference would it make whether the tale had been true or not? Truth could steal the imagination, give an unwanted ending that took away forever any add-to. Good stories were what you wanted them to be, a world in which perception was reality. Whether it came as truth or tall tale, she seemed pleased that his grandfather was telling instead of pining; letting out stories and old tales that had been cooped up inside him too long. Better that Nathan encourage him to let them out.

But it was the occasional tease that Nathan caught from his grandfather that pleased her the most. Judging humor the better cure, she encouraged Nathan to bear up with it since it brought no harm. She reminded him that his grandfather had at one time been considered the wittiest man on the mountain and could himself give or take. She opined as to how she and Nathan's father had caught their share of teasings from him and lived through it, often laughing about it now from time to time. Teasings were mountain-made. And catching! Most men-made.

With the nights still cold enough for a fire, Nathan went of the evenings to split wood and to see that the wood-box near the Franklin stove inside the cabin was filled for the night. Often while he split the wood, his grandfather would tell him to size up a block of wood before splitting it. Sized right, one could almost stare the wood into splitting; or be certain of no more than one blow from the ax. A splitting ax should have a dull end so as not to stick in the wood. Hickory was the best wood of all, while locust would burn next to coal. All fruitwoods were prized, although his grandfather did not choose to burn them because he had been told by his own father that burning fruitwood would bring bad luck. The mountain was hard enough living without adding-to.

Nathan drew and kept fresh well water inside the cabin, and from time to time brought a cooked meal that his mother had fixed and asked Nathan to coax his grandfather to accept. But Nathan soon learned that coaxing was useless: he either would or wouldn't, and gave no reason. Nathan's mother, instead of seeming offended, took pleasure in knowing of his independence. She set the food back for another time, or if it wouldn't keep, added it to her compost pile or fed it to birds and wild animals.

Even when his grandfather chose to accept the plate, he always fussed about it, considering it a show of dependence to accept but tempering his fussing with a grin, claiming that next to Nathan's grandmother, his mother was the best cook on the mountain. And, why not? Hadn't she learned the most of it from Nathan's grandmother!

Given a choice, his grandfather seemed to enjoy cooking his own meals on the Franklin stove. Amidst the sweet smell and lessons learned on how to fry rabbits and squirrels and the like, Nathan listened to stories told, wondering how so many memories could be cooped up inside the small, withered body of his grandfather. It seemed hard to believe that time could have stolen away so much of the man he had once been. At times the stories were so scary that Nathan made excuses to spend the night at the cabin, careful in not letting his grandfather know how scared he was. He told Nathan superstitions, beliefs, and omens that came with the mountain; to believe them cost nothing, but not to believe and be wrong cost everything.

Since Nathan had become his mother's source of information concerning his grandfather, he was often asked to repeat stories and conversations that breeched no secrets between the two. She seemed concerned most over the continued memory loss; stories trailing off without endings. She did not elaborate, but Nathan saw it in her eyes and in the rubbing of her hands. She reminded Nathan of the need to listen, to accept what his grandfather gave without questioning or asking for left-outs. Seeing concern on Nathan's face, she spoke of good signs, like fussing over the food she sent and the color that was coming back to his skin. He should give his grandfather his own pace without inquiring. The coming spring could be the telling season. Hopefully a rebirth for the good of all.

And so it was on a day in early spring that Nathan's grandfather spoke to him about working the land again. He had set his thoughts on a piece of bottomland along the creek below the cabin and suggested they scout it out. During the trip there he spoke of the need to check out the condition of the plow and harrow stored under the shed near the cabin.

Back at the cabin Nathan's grandfather brought out a small box that he had stored away. A box that held seed. He fondled a sack of eight-row corn and smaller pinches of redheart tomatoes, cabbage, and pepper, as well as an assortment of seed for greens and turnips. It was time now for Nathan to learn to make his living off the mountain, so as never to become a burden to, or dependent on, others. These were the secrets his grandfather would pass on to him.

They went now to the shed to check on the bottom plow,

tooth harrow, and rastus cultivator that Nathan and his father had brought from his grandfather's place soon after his grandmother's death, using Sam and a drag sled to carry them. Nathan noticed that the points on the turning plow and rastus cultivator had been greased down to prevent rusting over the winter. Knowing that he or his father had not done this, he knew his grandfather had. It hurt that he was not asked to help or allowed to know.

At the shed now, his grandfather touched the handles of the rastus plow, pulling it upright while telling with pride how he had ordered it brought all the way upriver from Louisville. It had been the first of its kind on the mountain, a godsend for cultivating a garden. He told Nathan how it was better never to loan a plow, cultivator, or mule. And then, satisfied that everything was garden-fit, he called Sam up from the pasture and watched as the old mule made his way to the shed, slow and methodical. Nathan watched his grandfather rub the mule's nose, whispering to him that it was time for them to go to work again. He pointed for Nathan to look into the eyes of the old mule and see how excited he was, how happy Sam would be about earning his keep. While Nathan saw nothing but time in the eyes, he allowed his grandfather saw more. Nathan's grandmother had said that if Sam had not been a mule, she would have been jealous of their closeness, and that with their love for one another they also had in common a touch of orneriness and trying ways. As he talked, Nathan hoped he could not see how excited he was to tell his mother what his grandfather had said. That he had spoken of his grandmother without tears for the first time that he could recall. And had laughed instead.

When Nathan's father came home on the weekend, the four of them, counting the mule, went to the bottom to plow. They hauled the single bottom plow and a-harrow on a sled that Sam pulled with no strain. The rastus plow would be brought down later when time came for cultivating weeds and loosening the soil for rain. While Nathan's father sized up the field at the coaxing of his grandfather, who wanted to see that his teaching had not been forgotten, his grandfather hooked the plow to the singletree. He would cut the g-line through the center of the field so they could plow both going and coming and save time and mule-work. They could share then with the rest of the plowing, dividing furrows. The land was rich and soft owing much to Sourwood Creek, which had carried the topsoil from the mountain and deposited it here during high water. A land as black and soft as a rain cloud.

Both his grandfather and his father spoke of the creek, of its closeness and handiness for carrying water to water tomatoes and other small plantings during times of drought. They spoke of the need to rock across a shallow to dam up and hold enough water during dry spells to sink a bucket into. And then, while spelling the mule, they walked to the creek to scout it out. Nathan listened to the hum of the water over the rocks and wondered how far away it was that the creek first worked its way from the underside of the mountain. He had often dreamed of one day following it to its visible end, to watch it seep out of the earth. And along the way to check out the pools that held water even in dry weather. Some holes he knew now, holes where sizable bass and catfish lived. He stared at small minnows so transparent that he could see through them to their tails. He saw a handful of crawdads that still carried their winter shells, brownish-black from cold water. And he knew when the weather warmed enough they would swim to the edge of the bank to shed, their bodies soft to the touch and limp enough to fold over a finger. He would gather them to take home to eat and also to fish with. He reckoned how only worms matched a soft crawdad for catching fish.

Taking turns now holding the plow, Nathan thought that Sam was even smarter when it came to gardening than his grandfather had claimed. Given his way, he could teach. He knew how far to go, and when to make his turn either left or right. Nathan soon learned that if you did not give him his way, he would take it. He also was soon learning—to his embarrassment in front of his father and grandfather—that a mule would indeed test you. Sam refused to go when Nathan took the plow. Paid no attention to his mule-talk whatsoever. And did so until, following instructions from his grandfather, Nathan was able to make Sam go. Even then he would have sworn that while his grandfather whispered what to do as Nathan plowed his way up the field, Sam had turned his ears backwards to hear what his grandfather was saying, and changed to please him. He plowed then with the worry that Sam's going had not been Nathan's showing who was boss at all, but his grandfather's want.

Whichever, Nathan plowed with a pride he had never known. And words of encouragement and approval from his grandfather as he made his turn, that he was born to a mule man, made it even more so. A chip off of not one but two blocks! In the end he learned that Sam was the greatest teacher of all, knowing when to work and knowing when to stop to rest, which tempered tiredness.

After the plowing, with the a-harrow hooked to the singletree, Nathan got to ride the combination tooth harrow disk-drag to help hold it to the land while it pulverized and smoothed the soil for planting. Shifting the dirt, worms were often brought to the surface, and Nathan, given a can and instructions from his father before- hand, carefully pinched the worms out from between the teeth of the harrow to use later for fishing; fish that his grandfather had prom- ised to fry on top of the Franklin stove, adding touches of butter that Nathan had churned from the Jersey's milk. Milk so heavy with but- terfat that it could have been spooned off. His grandfather had ladled the churned butter into a wooden butter mold he had whittled out of buckeye, carving pictures of flowers on the bottom and underside of the lid to print off into the butter, making it pretty to look at. He had chosen the mold that Nathan's grandmother had liked the best, a cluster of forget-me-nots. That he had chosen to use it and talk about it to Nathan had been another good sign, according to his mother; to do so without crying, a promise.

After the field had been plowed, at the coaxing of his grandfather they left the field to lie fallow, to wait out a rise that might come to the creek from heavy rains. Too often, according to his grandfather, garden land, especially along a creek, was planted too early, only to be washed out or wasted standing in water. To plant early or wait until later was always a gamble. Planting early was best; planting late was often to miss early rains and end up with a drought in July when growth was needed. But his grandfather did not have seed to waste and chose not to gamble.

It was during their waiting that word came that a family by the name of Hawkins had moved into the old vacant Dillard farm over the mountain from Nathan's. Land where Nathan's grandfather hunted when he was a boy, even up to taking Nathan's father with him. His grandfather felt the urge to see it again now that an excuse for going had come. They should make the trip over the mountain to meet their new neighbors and see if they needed anything while settling in.

Thinking that the trip might be good for Nathan's grandfather and would give Nathan a chance to see more of the mountain, as well as being a neighborly thing to do, his mother gave them some canned goods to take along for a gift. She was pleased that after so long a time they would have neighbors, even though the distance was nearly a half-day's ride over rough land. The Dillards had been gone longer than she could remember without searching for reminders. Whispering cautions to Nathan concerning the long journey his grandfather would be making at his age, she bade them a safe trip.

Leading Sam to a rise in the land by the house to shorten the distance for mounting, his grandfather placed the sack holding what Nathan's mother was sending over the mule's neck and, with his bony hand, steadied Nathan as he climbed up behind him. Once out of hearing, he reminded Nathan that it was a woman's way to find worry where there was none, and that he had known the ways of the mountain before she had been born but knew she meant well.

The Hawkins had moved into the two-story home where the Dillards once lived, which front-faced a small branch, its backside and first floor penned to the hill, the top floor not touching. This side of it, his grandfather pointed out to him some shawnee greens good for eating and some witch's bells for a heart remedy; both had been brought from farther up the mountain for closeness in time of need. The Dillards had been smart people, knowing the mountain.

They were met in the yard by Mrs. Hawkins and were told that Mr. Hawkins had gone off to see about steady work at a coal mine over on Martha, a half-day's ride from there. Taking the sack that Nathan's mother had sent, she handed it to her daughter, whom she introduced as Rennie, their only child but good around the house. Rennie seemed embarrassed by the tacking-on and did not look at either Nathan or his grandfather when introduced. If she had chosen to look, Nathan thought he might not have taken a chance to see she was red-headed, with freckles to match. She stood there with her head lowered, her hands clasped together in front of her. She swayed from side to side. Afraid that his grandfather might catch his stare and use it as a tease on their way back over the mountain, he looked away, but not before he judged her about his own age and for some reason wished she were a boy.

Nathan worried that as he turned his head his grandfather had caught her staring up at him. He had seen her out of a corner of an eye. When Mrs. Hawkins asked her to draw fresh water from the well and bring the gourd for drinking, his grandfather made matters worse by asking Nathan to help her draw the water, being as the bucket was so large and heavy for a girl but not for a boy as strong as Nathan. Embarrassed, he took his grandfather's shooing-off, dismounted, and walked to the well, making sure that he did not stare at her along the way. Looking out over the mountain instead, he tripped once and was more embarrassed than ever.

They did not stay long. Mrs. Hawkins said she could not be sure how steady the work would be at the mine for Mr. Hawkins, if at all, but if long enough to make a crop she would get word to them about needing seed. Nathan's grandfather spoke of the school in Sourwood, how he judged Rennie and Nathan might be in the same grade and that he was sure Nathan would be of help to her. He was awfully smart at book ciphering. Reminding her that turnips and greens could be planted as far along as late July, Nathan's grandfather turned back over the mountain, Nathan chancing to see that Rennie stared after them. He thought that, girl or boy, loneliness was the same. How before his grandfather had come to live so close that he had known it, too.

Just as Nathan had been afraid might happen, his grandfather teased about Rennie, how pretty she was. Then his talk turned to how she was about the same age as Nathan's grandmother when his grandfather had first laid eyes on her during a visit not so unlike the one they had made today. His grandmother, too, had had freckles, freckles that he learned all too soon she would not take a tease over. And how later he had returned to court and then marry her. He had not been able to see his grandfather's face, riding backside, but with his arms around his waist, he had known how hard the telling had been by his grandfather's breathing, that his grandfather was holding back a cry.

Later in the day after returning home and building nerve to do so, Nathan told his mother of the teasing he had taken over Rennie. Looking to see that his grandfather was out of hearing and sight, she laughed and said that menfolk were bad to tease when it came to girls and worse for some reason on those who had freckles. That she, too, had had freckles growing up and had taken her share of teasing. Even from Nathan's father until she had taught him better. That teasing was the best sign yet when it came to his grandfather, and with no harm done and teasing being a part of mountain men, he should let it go at that and be pleased over the progress his grandfather was making. She added that neither he nor his grandfather looked the worse after making such a long trip over the mountain and back.

Within two weeks after he and his grandfather had made the trip, Nathan's father brought word that the Hawkins were moving. The job Mr. Hawkins had hoped for had not worked out, the seam of coal in the new mine not proving workable. He heard that Mr. Hawkins had decided to follow the mine as far away as Elkhorn and had probably moved by now. Nathan had not come to know them enough to miss them and thought their moving should bring an end to the teasing over Rennie, so he made sure his grandfather knew about it by mentioning it to him on several occasions, none of which his grandfather acknowledged. But Nathan now credited a reason to their work in the garden and his grandfather's enthusiasm for it, for the time had come to plant the eight-row corn, and much work was to be done.

Marking rows three feet apart, with Nathan going up one row and staying even with his grandfather in the next row, they planted corn three feet apart in each row. They made hills by scooping out shallow holes with a gooseneck hoe, dropping in five seeds, and then covering them no more than two inches deep. This was the way his grandfather had learned from his father and his father's father before him. Five seeds allowed for a sure break and growth of three stalks. If all of the seed germinated, they would thin back to three. But not until the corn had grown enough to cheat the crows and blackbirds that came to the field after the corn had sprouted. They would come to steal whenever the corn broke ground, tiny spear-like shoots that turned the top of the land green to a seasoned eye. This was the stage the birds chose. They liked to dig with their bills into the earth to find the soft seed that clung to the tiny root hairs. Once the corn was farther along and any show of seed gone, the birds would leave. They would not return until the corn was earring out.

As hard and slow as the work was, Nathan enjoyed every moment of it. From planting, to sprouting, and then coming to scare the birds away. He learned that nothing came free on the mountain and that sharing was something you had to do, whether you wanted to or not. You could not ladle out how much the birds and varmints such as muskrats and coons would eat or where in the field they chose to eat. Neither, he learned, had knowledge of being wasteful, often peeling down the end of an ear and leaving it open for cornworms and beetles to gather in or the weather to ruin. Truth was, according to his grandfather, they knew nothing of stealing, only that what they found on the mountain was theirs to do with as they pleased. They had been with the mountain longer than Nathan or his grandfather. Nathan watched the corn from sprouting to the stay roots that came to anchor it from the wind.

It was after the corn had grown tall enough to turn the wind into music that Nathan's grandfather first mentioned the cornstalk fiddle. It had been the cornstalk fiddle that won the heart of Nathan's grandmother, a mountain magic they shared with one another for better than seventy years. It had also been the cornstalk fiddle that he had taught Nathan's father to make and play that had won the heart of Nathan's mother. A fiddle he had learned to play from his own father and had handed down to Nathan's father. He laughed while he told of how it had been with Nathan's father, making the fiddle to catch music inside the stalk of corn. How long the wait until the corn caught the music of the rain, wind, and sun, and finally moonwine aged through the limbs of a great black oak tree at the edge of the field. He told how Nathan's father had met Nathan's mother at a church social and had made plans to court her, plans that he thought were secret but were leaked out by his eyes and actions. How he had grown restless knowing that Eb Dillard's boy, Ceph, had his eyes set on Nathan's mother also. Eb also grew a fine strip of corn and knew how to make cornstalk fiddles to catch a girl.

It had come down that year to who was able to find the sweetest stalk of corn in the field, one with the most music, and learn how to play it better than the other. Unbeknownst to either Nathan's father or Ceph, he and Eb had known about it and placed a bet as to who would win. The loser had agreed to shock the other's field of corn. A secret that they were bound to keep. In the end, Nathan's father had won hands down. When Eb came to shock the field of corn, it was taken only as a neighborly thing to do. Shocked the field while Nathan's grandfather pretended to be helping but all the while fishing at his favorite hole at a creek.

The story too good to keep, Nathan had asked his mother about the truth of it. She frowned as if trying to remember and then grinned recalling that she had heard his grandfather tell of winning his grandmother's heart with a cornstalk fiddle. How back then the cornstalk fiddle was the only fiddle they had, being so far off into the mountain. It had been handed down to Nathan's father more, she thought, to keep a mountain custom and old men's dreams of a past alive. She recalled how Nathan's father had come that first evening playing a cornstalk fiddle that screeched like a pond full of swamp frogs. The next evening, Ceph Dillard had come with one that squeaked like a dry well pulley. She had chosen Nathan's father not because of a cornstalk fiddle that he had been put up to by his father to play but for other reasons that a girl chooses a boy for. Among them, looks, manners, and being a good provider for a family.

Nathan's mother was more pleased by this than anything else, that his grandfather had spoken of making a cornstalk fiddle, that he was choosing to talk about love instead of pining his life away over it. With memories a love is forever. This was the most encouraging sign since Nathan's grandmother had died, and unless Nathan disagreed, she would like to share the news with Nathan's father. To ease the worry he now carried with him every day. Nathan should be happy about it too. And she encouraged him to watch and learn the makings of a cornstalk fiddle, if for no other reason than to please his grandfather. While there was no medicine on the mountain to cure what his grandfather was ailing from, the fiddle might just be the closest thing.

By the time the weather changed enough to brown the corn until it rattled in the wind, Nathan's grandfather had become obsessed with the making of the cornstalk fiddle. He took great pains in telling and showing Nathan how it should be made and how he was to practice until he could play it. He spoke now of the Hawkins and how they might make another trip over there to see if help was needed and if Rennie was getting ready for school. He spoke as if they had never moved at all. And then, making matters worse, he talked as if the Dillards were still there, not the Hawkins at all. About their fine stand of corn and Eb's plans to teach Ceph how to make a cornstalk fiddle. Nathan kept this a secret, not wanting to worry his mother.

He listened and watched closely when it came to making the cornstalk fiddle. And it seemed to please his grandfather. He helped him render some pitch to rosin a bow and went with him to select the stalk of corn. The search for it was narrowed to two hills near the creek, hills that his grandfather had had him water over dry spells. Nathan had not known the reason until now and was hurt that his grandfather had not chosen to share it at the time.

The stalk selected, his grandfather cut out a section of it that included two joints. He then cut strings from within the two joints. This he did carefully, making lengthwise cuts between the joints just under the fiber, which became the strings. Nathan watched his grandfather trim out the excess stalk underneath the first cut, making a hollow area. He trimmed again the excess stalk between the strings, leaving enough fiber to make four strings. Then he cut a bridge out of a thin piece of cedar and made notches for the strings, a bridge he stretched under the strings under tension but without breaking. He then made a bow from a sliver of cornstalk.

The fiddle finished, Nathan practiced. In between, he went back to the cornfield to shuck corn. He needed to gather what they had not eaten or pickled to feed Sam during the winter.

Still Nathan did not choose to tell his mother how much worse his grandfather's memory had become. His own world seemed to have turned upside down. Sometimes he thought that she knew. More than once he had heard her crying softly in her bedroom, thinking he was asleep. Especially after she had made trips to the cabin, dismissive of her reasons for going.

As Nathan practiced now, his grandfather spoke of making a bet, a bet that just might get their field of corn shocked without them having to cut a stalk but instead lazying off fishing in the creek. Worrying over his grandfather's mind changing so much now, Nathan still kept it secret, especially after his grandfather had caught himself forgetting once and drew a promise from Nathan to keep it a secret. Nathan took his spite out on the cornstalk fiddle; he had come to both love and hate it. Love for what it had once meant to his grandfather, and hate for what it seemed to be doing to him now. Especially at night after practice, never getting beyond squeaks like his mother had said, but ones that drew praise and approval from his grandfather, he looked through the window to see his grandfather sitting on the bed crying softly, the fiddle in one hand and a picture of his grandmother in the other. At times on his leaving, his grandfather had called him by his father's name.

Early one evening when Nathan had returned from feeding out and had gone to practice, he saw his grandfather sitting in the chair holding the cornstalk fiddle and bow in his hand. He motioned for Nathan to come closer and, when he did, handed him the fiddle and bow. Leaning his head forward, he whispered, "It's time for you to go to the Dillards now."

Taking the fiddle and bow and holding them in the crook of his arm, Nathan turned and walked slowly toward the mountain.

Girty

Growing up, we called her Girty. For those of us who still remember, we still do. It didn't seem important back then that she had a last name. It still doesn't, although I have since learned that her last name was Barton.

Girty lived in a world of hearsay, especially among boys. The older around Sourwood were never willing to talk about her other than to say she was a child-woman, having the body of a woman but the mind of the child. She was a warning and a brag. A warning for young girls not to be like; a brag for boys who tried to use her as a growing-up mark, mysterious and exciting. But mostly for us she was someone to imagine but not touch. I did not believe then, and I don't now, that there was a thread of truth to any brag I ever heard. Even so, that never took away the thrill of listening.

According to hearsay, she was born in a cave in Viny Branch, a spur hollow carved out of Sourwood Mountain. Starting as a spring from the underside of the mountain, over time it had dug out and carried its way for better than a quarter mile before it emptied into the Sourwood River. Like the other creeks that snaked out of the mountain, it was peaceful during dry weather but hell-to-pay during wet. The sides of the hollow were so steep on either side that, if not for fox grapes and muscadines that roped the rim, the sides would have been impossible to hold on to. From the bed of the hollow everything seemed to lean over you.

Her mother had died during childbirth, leaving just Girty and her father living together in the cave. It was said that Girty's father buried his wife outside the mouth of the cave in a shallow grave that varmints later dug up and destroyed, with no place left to mourn or hold flowers. Her father was a no-good and walked with a limp, having broken a leg once when thrown from a coal-drag. Without a proper set, the leg had mended crooked, which left it shorter than the other. He seldom worked and only then as a means of buying whiskey. He was a drunkard, mean and overbearing. Especially to Girty. Hearsay was that he beat her and used her in ways that we were not permitted to talk about, except when we were alone at campfires at night. And then, the older among us claiming to have witnessed such things told stories that were sad but exciting. Boys were like that; still are.

Her father had died when she was eight or nine, and he was buried in a pauper's grave in Sourwood Cemetery with no mourners. There was a superstition on the mountain that when evil people died, the devil chased them out of the grave and around the cemetery on the first night before catching them and pulling them down forever. So boys gathered that night to watch his grave. And they told stories too scary to listen to: how he moaned and groaned as he laced through tombstones trying to escape the devil's fork and losing in the end. His moans had been left to the wind and even now on certain nights could be heard if you had enough nerve to go listen, which I did not have then or now.

Some of the boys said that on the night of his burial they had caught a glimpse of Girty hid-off in the brush. After the undertaker had left, she had stolen flowers from a grave nearby and placed them over his grave. Whether she did or not, from that day forth she caught the blame for all flowers stolen or wind-claimed on the cemetery. And for flowers that had never been in the first place.

After her father's death she moved out of the cave to live with an old haint-of-a-woman in a two-room stilt house that hung like a crooked picture frame on the high banks of the river. She was said to earn her board by watching after the old woman.

When I was old enough to run with the younger boys and pester the older, the cave fascinated me, and I went there often either with others or alone. Deserted except for hunters who used it to cheat snow or rain or to break a cold wind, it was lonesome and storyish. A place to sit and imagine.

The floor of the cave was finger-thick with dust, weather-ground and thin enough to be tossed into the wind like smoke. Ant lions had doodled into it, and acorns pushed grave-mounds above the surface. Acorns that I scratched out, believing Girty had played with them as a child instead of their being carried in by a squirrel. For it was said that growing up she had used acorns to make dolls and to thread necklaces. She had loved dolls but had never owned one store-bought.

Imagining her there, I listened to the weird music of the wind that played the mouth of the cave like a flute, a haunting song of loneliness almost too sad to bear. I imagined her threading the acorns using thorns as needles, living on wild game she caught from deadfalls and wild berries and grapes that she gathered. I thought of how wonderful and beautiful the mountain was in spring and autumn, a forever-life of no schooling and no bathing except in the creek or from a rain-made waterfall over the mouth of the cave. I thought of winters and loneliness and a stillness that settled over the land. I would not have wanted to live in the cave year-round.

Once Girty left the hollow, she grew up living in the stilt house and walking the single railroad tracks that hauled coal out of the Sourwood Valley from upriver. Mostly, this part of the world was hers alone, keeping her away from the streets of town and people close up. It furnished what little money she made to live on by gathering coal that had fallen off the coal-cars on their way downriver to be loaded on barges and shipped by water to places unknown. She had been quick to learn that when coal did not fall on its own, she could help it along by catching and climbing the ladder on each of the cars and throwing off enough to keep without bringing trouble.

She sold or bartered coal hereabouts for little-to-nothing, delivering it at back doors at night in a world as black as the coal.

Girty chewed tobacco, and she kept a short twist of burley gleaned from the few burley bases around Sourwood in a small cloth pouch tied around her neck. She could spit ambeer through the eye of a needle, missing nothing she spurted at, which was boys, mostly. She walked the tracks with a sway, gorilla-like, her long arms, especially when she leaned, almost touching the ground. Her leaning caused her breasts to fall out of her loose dress, giving the boys something exciting to talk about. She fought to keep them covered, stuffing them back inside the thin dress like they were more of a pester than a purpose. If she knew we watched, she never let on. Lem Daniels claimed he had been close enough once to see that her breasts were freckled like a bird's egg. Others said they looked the same as the ones on the other women in town who stopped while shopping to breastfeed a baby—something that we were forbidden to watch but did. Forbidden to build brags on but did, being boys.

In time, word of her breasts spread over the town, and some women in Sourwood set about to stop it. They approached Judge Bolten and demanded that something be done. Holding an elective office and being vote-wise, Judge Bolten turned the case over to his constable, Homer Dalton.

Said to have a brain the size of a pea drought-grown, Homer also had a little woman, jealous and mean as a warhorse hen. Smelling trouble with his little woman right off and knowing that Girty could fight like a man, spit through the eye of a needle, and bark a squirrel with a railroad rock, he asked Judge Bolten how he might carry out the order. To which Judge Bolten told him that, first off, he would have to look for the evidence. As to how he could get by his woman on something like that, the judge told him to pray, to run like hell, but to lose no votes if he wanted to keep his job.

Homer hid-off in the spirea bushes that lined both sides of the railroad tracks, bushes that had been planted long ago by the railroad company to appease the town for stealing some of its beauty away with raised land and steel rails. Over the years they had grown unkempt and rank but in spring remained a showcase of white flowers. Bushy and jungle-like, they were our hiding place when Girty walked the tracks. But also a devil for getting tangled in and caught. Like Tom Stamper had once done. Hitting Girty with a rock, he had turned to run and got trapped in new growth. She had landed on top of him, straddling him, he later said, with legs as white and soft as the belly of a channel cat. He said nothing about her fist that put the knots on his face. But he bragged about how fighting hadn't been all that happened while they were tangled up. What had happened had been worth the knots. But no one believed him enough to gamble on.

If Homer saw the evidence that day, no one ever knew. That he carried a lump on his jaw big as a goose egg was common knowledge. Whether he caught it from his little woman or from Girty belonged to the imagination of the teller.

By the time Girty had grown woman-size, she had become ugly and almost as smelly as the stockyard on the south end of Sourwood—fair game for us all. Truth was, we treated her like a wild animal. Unhuman-like. Our world was to "get Girty," with no whys attached. She was our way to a brag; for the women in town, the way to a sin. Brother Mayhall preached that she was devil-sent, though some members of the congregation were not willing to go quite that far. Yet no one offered help that we knew of. She ate what she could find in nature or garbage cans and wore what had been thrown away. Of the winter, she wrapped her feet in old newspapers and built fires from coal along the tracks for warmth and to eat by. Tearing at food like an animal while we watched from the spireas and conjured up ways to make life more miserable for her.

The year World War II began, by accident I hit Girty with a rock. For some strange reason I had never wanted to hit her but, unbeknownst to others, had thrown to be accepted by them, to pretend that I threw for a brag. But this day I threw a flat railroad rock that had caught the wind, curved, and caught her above her right eye. I knew that it stung and that others had seen. She shook her head like she was trying to shake off the pain that had landed there. She was bleeding heavily. For some strange reason I had never thought of her bleeding, that she would be like us.

And then, with her eyes, she picked me out of the spirea bush. Too petrified to run now, I stared back. She made no move to catch me, but stared with eyes that seemed to search for the reason I had hit her. I wondered if she could see in my eyes how sorry I was that I had thrown the rock. And then she hiked up a corner of her dress to wipe the blood from her right eye. She wore nothing under the dress, and I felt a boy gouge me and whisper to the others. For the other boys it was a time for watching not throwing, even though she was a still target instead of a moving one like she generally was. I saw her trying to wince away the pain. I still do.

I became the end of a brag. Not only for scoring a bull's-eye with the rock, but for the hiking of the dress.

At nights I relived throwing the rock over and over again. I saw Girty trying to shake the pain, wincing and throwing blood on the train tracks. I tried to think of ways to make amends and then worried that the other boys might learn of it. I was caught between two worlds. I had made a scar on the both of us that would never heal. I lived a brag by day, a nightmare by night. Life was miserable. Especially since the way it turned out, I lost any chance of making amends.

I had gone into Sourwood in December to see if ice had frozen thick enough along the edges of Sourwood River to ice-skate.

I was sure some other boys would be there also. Just this side of the riverbank I saw several boys heading down the brick road that followed the river. I hurried to catch up, and when I did Ned Hurley told me that someone had been knocked off the railroad trestle by a coal-drag and thrown some fifty feet below where the tracks crossed Sourwood Creek.

By the time we reached the trestle, a crowd from town had gathered and was making its way slowly down the bank to see who it was. Joining them, I thought I heard someone say that it was only Girty, as if to offer some relief.

And so it was. She lay there crumpled in an awkward position among rocks and creek muck, bleeding from her ears, nose, mouth, and places on her body. Her eyes were closed, and her worn, thin skirt was hiked above her waist. She wore nothing underneath, and her legs were spread, exposing her nakedness. Girls blushed and looked away.

Finally, a woman said, "My God, won't someone have the common decency to cover her up!"

For what seemed like an eternity, no one moved. And then a girl-child no older than eight or nine scurried from the crowd and ran toward Girty. She carried a small rag doll in her arms. Taking one hand, she pulled Girty's skirt down, turned to go, and then turned to Girty again. Bending down, she placed the rag doll in the crook of Girty's arm and then disappeared into the crowd.

With no one to mourn and sit up with her, Girty was buried the same day in a pauper's grave in the Sourwood Cemetery. I never heard any mention that boys had gone there to see if the devil chased her from the grave that first night. For it was believed here on the mountain that people like Girty, with a child's mind, had been promised a place by the Almighty. Whether she was buried with the doll I never knew. But I hoped so. The mountain is a lonely place.

To Plant
a Windsong

Hattie Milton was said to be a witch among the boys on Sourwood Mountain. For as long as could be remembered, she had
been the age-set for growing up and the high mark for making
brags. Growing up was gauged by the degree of belief in her witchery, and brags by the distance she could cast a spell and your brav-
ery in being the closest in range.

Among the youngest she was a witch, pure and simple. They
believed everything. In older boys, shadows of doubt crept in re-
garding some of her powers, and on these doubts small brags had
set in. The oldest boys, more so during the daylight hours, scoffed
at being afraid yet claimed enough to scare and make life miserable for all the others. They walked around independent-like with
their chests stuck out, building brags that ranged from molehills to
mountain size.

But brags were hard to come by, being dependent on her
trance-like casting out of spells and on the nerve to be within range
of whatever she chose to cast. Brags generally came on two occa-

sions: one was to hawk her during the few trips she made out of the head of the hollow where she lived to fetch things at Ned Hewlett's store, and the other was to crawl down the side of the mountain above her cabin to spy on her. Escape her wrath and bring back something believable, and you had a mountain-size brag in the making! And with little chance that it would ever be challenged. To do that meant following the bragger's footsteps and making it back alive. And everyone knew the old mountain saying, "The first one excites the snake, the second one gets bit."

All of the boys were in agreement that she had every attribute of a witch. She was properly yoked with scary tales, omens, superstitions, and past doings to prove. Wherever boys gathered they added to: around hunt fires, at Sourwood School, and along the river. Many were passed on by the old men who set the day to whittle at Ned Hewlett's store, of the summer on a bench he kept out front, or of the winter by the fire in the potbellied stove inside. Truth was, tales from the old men were the scariest of the lot. And they sought boys out like a spider does a fly. The nearer dark and farther the distances, the scarier the tale.

To begin with, Hattie was an old woman, which was witch-making in itself. According to older boys and the whittlers down at Ned Hewlett's, men did not turn into witches. And she lived alone up the longest, dampest, night-darkest, and scariest hollow on Sourwood Mountain. Married at an early age, she was widowed when her man Henry died long after from mysterious reasons. She buried him in her yard, and witchgrass had quickly grown over his mound and spread to the land close-in. Witchgrass was a witch-mark, a grass too bothersome to be natural, bad to spread and choking out all other grasses including flowers. It was said that the prints of her knees could be seen in the grass from the nights when the moon was full and like a ball of fire over the mountain, when she knelt rocking back and forth beside the grave mound mumbling words to her dead husband in an unknown tongue that only the dead could hear and cipher. Since none of the boys ever had nerve to visit the cabin this close up, this tale had been carried-in.

Witch-like, she was a shadow of a woman, back-bowed, sunken eyes crow-footed and black as a buzzard's wing. Her hair was grey and thin as strands of a spider's web, catching the wind feeble-like.

How far she could see or hear was attached to age among the boys on the mountain. The younger believed she could hear and see all, with distance playing no part. The in-betweens shortened the distance a little on both but leaving room to run. The older boys cut the distances close enough to scare and pin a brag. Brags on how close-in they had crept down the sides of either ridge above her cabin at night to spy on her.

Leantoe Thomas held the bigger of the brags when it came to creeping down the mountainside. He claimed he had sneaked so close to the cabin one night, and the ridge had become so steep, that he had had to hook a toe around a sassafras sapling to keep from sliding into her yard and being exposed. To prove it he had cut a notch in the bark of the sapling for anyone to go see. No one had built the nerve to challenge him, not for truth or a chance to build a bigger brag. They were willing to give him top brag and pinned him his nickname, Leantoe Thomas.

Helping to round her out witch-proper were tales of a cow and cat she kept. The cow was a muley, a yellow Jersey muley to boot. And who doubted that a milk cow had to have horns or be spell-marked? Sid Ramey's dad worked at the Sourwood Stock-yard, and he claimed that a muley cow was a cow hit by the worst sort of witchcraft, sad and burdensome to carry. Not only did Hattie Milton's cow have no horns, but that every calf she had thrown had been a muley also. Crippled in a left hind leg, witch-sent, the cow spent the days nibbling for food with old teeth among the briars and scrub brush on the steep sides of the mountain, taking off more weight than what she grubbed adding on. He judged her too old now for calf-bearing and had heard-say that Hattie had turned her dry far back, Hattie claiming that her hands had become too arthritic to milk her any longer. Working around cows at the stockyard made Mr. Ramey cow-smart, and no one doubted his word. Anyway, it was too good a story not to believe.

The big cat she owned was bobtailed and said to be crossed up with a bobcat. Yellow striped, it was bigger than a red fox and meaner than a rattler. It roamed the mountain mostly at nights and, Hattie-sent, searched for stray boys or slow hounds. Often at nights the big cat's wailing cry could be heard on the mountain, mournful as a lost soul. Rumor was the cat's name was Lucifer and that it had sent many a hound back to the fox fire with a tail between its legs. Or, if caught, the hound never came back at all. No one on Sourwood Mountain dared hunt varmints up near Hattie Milton's cabin, day or night. Word was the cat would come after you! There was no way to know what Hattie had put it up to do.

With her crippled cow and crossed-up cat, Hattie was said to spend her time sitting on the cabin porch thinking of things to cast spells on and mixing up a concoction, a witch's brew she made from henbane gathered along the mountain. When the moon was in the proper stage, she mixed the brew with bat's blood, snakes that Lucifer drug in, toads, and the fat from a dead chicken she had killed with a curse. Tales too scary not to believe, too scary to miss! One sip and you joined the chicken!

Old people on the mountain, mainly the women, saw Hattie Milton differently. And among these women was Ishmael's mother. She tacked the witch tales to boys' wants and add-ons to old men who had little more gumption than to whittle their lives away on a bench in front of Ned Hewlett's or reddening behinds humped up to the potbellied stove. Casting blame on a woman when it was their trifling ways that led boys astray. Filled their heads with nonsense.

She set about to whittle off their tales one at a time. To begin with, Hattie's man Henry had not died in a mysterious way at all, like dying from a brew that Hattie had mixed from Witch's Bells to poison him. Knowing herbal remedies better than most on Sourwood Mountain, she had doctored him for years with Witch's Bells for his bad heart. But because of his stubbornness, in the end the rough land and scythe had claimed him.

Ishmael's mother told how the two of them, Hattie and Henry, had grown old together, had built their cabin where it still stood with their bare hands longer ago than most remembered. They had scratched out a living, she taking in washings and scrubbing them over a washboard until her fingers turned red and in time knotted like the claws of an old chicken. Henry had fought briars and brush, pushing them back on the steep sides of the ridges above the cabin until his health finally gave way. They had forever been on the small side, little people and winter-poor. Until the day his heart gave way he swore he would one day move Hattie out of the dark hollow to the lowlands along the Sourwood River where the land was so fertile you could make a crop anywhere you chose to drop the seed. He would grow enough grub to sell in Sourwood and would no longer have to hire out, and Hattie would not have to take in washings anymore.

He never made it. And she had him buried close because she refused to give him up even in death, and that was as far as they could get with him for her to consent to burial. This was not un-usual. Many burials were close enough to whisper to. She had kept him above ground as long as she could until he began to turn. His eyes would not close, and they put pennies over them. Buried, she had refused to leave his grave even though it was in the dead of winter. She slept beside the mound and refused to eat when others came to check on her and to feed her old cow and yellow cat until she was time-healed. She finally caught pneumonia, and if Ely Taylor hadn't found her lying across the mound and taken her to the cabin and brought in his woman to help, she would have died. Came near death anyway.

Once on her feet again she still chose to sit beside the grave, for love, not witchery. Mumbling to him in an unknown tongue wasn't unordinary. Didn't birds sing to one another? Didn't grouse

drum in the woods during the spring? And what about the bull-
frogs bellowing along the creek? Birds knew. Grouse knew. Frogs
knew. Hattie knew. Henry knew. Love between the two spoke of
something that didn't need to be understood by others it was not
intended for. To Ishmael's mother's way of thinking, if Hattie's
words could have been ciphered they would have been the softest,
sweetest words ever heard on Sourwood Mountain. Their love had
been that great.

"Beats all!" she fussed. "Old women making witches! Lord
knows if there was such a thing as a witch it would have to be a
man, most having more sneaking ways about them than berries on
a red cedar tree; more sweet lies than a hive of honey. Man wasn't
born without a tall tale and a lie tacked to him. Night whisperers
of sweet talk mostly."

Hattie had always been a good woman, and if the old men
down at Ned Hewlett's were whittling around scaring little boys
about her, or if the books down at Sourwood School had little
more to say than tales about witches, then she might just have to
make a trip down to both places and see about that! Hattie had
had more than her share of hard times on the mountain, and Sourwood had more than its share of superstitions and tall tales. The
mountain needed no tacking on by fancy books or long-tongued
men! Hattie Milton was a good woman, old and waiting her time
same as others old on Sourwood. Like others she had not been
promised another day. Hers was a world of sameness, a world in
which she had now become too feeble to make it out of the hollow
and depended on needs brought in.

Witch or not, Ishmael had made it through the last days of
school with his small brags and plans to prove something; brags
and plans made on the safe grounds of the schoolyard where the
boys gathered at recess trying to out-brag each other. And he might
have made it to summer if he had not chosen to stop with the
other boys to celebrate summer closing with a bottle of pop and a
piece of hard rock candy at Ned Hewlett's store, a ritual that took

place each year. But this day Ned Hewlett mentioned to them that Hattie Milton had sent word that she needed a boy big enough and with the know-how to plant the rich corn bottom along the creek below her cabin. Leif Potter would have the ground plowed, harrowed, and corn-ready for planting on Monday. And Ishmael, thinking he was among boys his own age, whisper-quiet struck a brag that topped the mountain and spread over far enough for the older boys to overhear him. They quickly brought the brag out into the open and exposed it to everyone.

Ishmael had dug his grave with his own tongue. A deep grave! Not only had he bragged that he would go to plant the corn, but he would cheat her by leaving at least some of the bottom fallow. To do so he would have to be close enough to her at the cabin for her to reach out and touch him! For him to smell and hear her voice! Chance life being snuffed out by as little a thing as a brag. A brag on Sourwood Mountain was never a take-back: once made it had to be kept or the bragger would be branded a coward forever, the brunt of finger-pointing and laughs from every gang of boys you passed forever and ever. Ned Hewlett cocooned his fate by telling everyone at the store that he would have Lief Potter take word to Hattie that Ishmael would be there on Monday by the time morning had broken.

Now, what had been a good day, the ending of school, turned into a nightmare! The closest Ishmael had ever been to Hattie Milton's cabin was a few feet down the slope from the top of the ridge, where shagbarks grew and the squirrels gathered to work on the hickory nuts in peace since boys were afraid to hunt or fire a shot. The shot would be heard by Hattie, and she would send a spell up the slope unseen to find you or by way of the yellow crossed-up bobcat to search you out. The few times she had been able to make it out of the hollow, Ishmael was never close. But like most of the boys younger and also his age, he was glad that she seldom if ever came now. Ned Hewlett had made arrangements with men like Lief Potter, who lived over the lip of the hollow beyond her cabin, to take provisions to her, and while there they chopped firewood for heat and cooking. She was alone on the mountain with little to do but grave-watch and conjure up ways to lay spells on boys without having to do much walking.

Ishmael knew that before the sun went down, word of his brag would have spread over the mountain. Even worse, if there could be a worse, he knew that boys would be making plans to watch him every step to the end of the brag, building ones of their own on how close they planned to be, the first one to see him snuffed out!

He said nothing about what happened to his mother when he reached home. But when he failed to eat supper she asked, "Everything go all right at school?"

He nodded his head and allowed he'd chop some kindling for the cookstove.

Sleep did not come until just this side of daylight. He had worried the night trying to figure why he had made such a brag, knowing full well what might be at the end of it; whether it might have been better to have owned up, backed down, and when he became older move on to where no one had ever heard of the brag he couldn't keep. He knew there was no chance the older boys would let up on his brag, and even the youngest would probably try to glean what little brag they could from it. To make matters worse he had no one to talk to about it and no way out. His life had dwindled down shorter than a school vacation, snuffed out in the end by his tongue.

On Saturday he gathered wood for a fire under the washtub so his mother could do her washing. Some things she boiled in hot water while he sliced slivers of homemade soap to drop in the water to cut the dirt. There had been a time when he had enjoyed slicing the soap, watching each sliver hit the water and rock itself under like leaves falling on the surface of Sourwood River. But not this day. He watched while she scrubbed the clothes over a washboard, which reminded him of how she had said Hattie Milton had washed over the heaved rows of metal until her fingers became gnarled like the claws of an old chicken. He stared at his mother's fingers red from the strong soap. He watched her separate colors into two tubs, hot and cold, so they would not fade. He would help her hang them on a long line stretched between black gums to catch the breeze coming in or out of the hollow.

Noticing his quietness, his mother swatted suds from her face and asked, "You feeling all right, Ishmael?" And then as if to add humor and cheer him up, she added, "Missing school?" She chuckled.

"Yes and no," he answered, wondering if a change had come to his voice, being so near what could be the end.

That evening he spent time on the hillside grubbing weeds around their garden, hoping to extend it beyond the onions, cabbage, and broccoli planted the highest on the slope. He thought how he had dreamed once and bragged to his mother how far up the slope he would one day clear for garden; produce for the house and enough left to peddle along with herbs and berries and the sort at Ned Hewlett's store. But this day as he grubbed, for some strange reason he thought of Henry Milton, how he had scythed his life away and was snuffed out either by grubbing or henbane. He thought of his trip come Monday to Hattie's cabin and what he would do if she offered him a brew to drink, coaxing that he needed it after the long trip up the hollow. He peered off along the slope now, not to ponder how far the garden could be extended, but to see if any boys had sneaked along the slope to watch him for whatever reason they chose—among them if physical changes were coming to one so near to the end, a short-timer on the mountain.

On Sunday matters grew worse. His mother had picked up his offer to plant Hattie Milton's corn, probably from one of the women at Sourwood church.

"I'm proud of you, Ishmael," she said. "I hope you won't charge her. Remember she only draws a little pension check. We have enough to make do."

When morning had broken on Monday and Ishmael was leaving on his way up the hollow, his mother said again, "Remember, truth is stronger than superstition!"

With charging for his work the least of his worries, Ishmael disappeared into the woods. He flinched when a grouse flushed up in front of him, and then a blue jay swung out of a black oak into the woods with its warning that he was coming. Normally he would have passed both happenings off. But for some reason as he made his way over the rugged land nothing seemed normal. Night-dew gathered on the limbs of trees during the night dripped now with the coming of day much louder than he could ever remember, making other sounds hard to pick up. Through the dripping dew he heard the hoot of an owl from deep in the hollow up ahead. He wondered why the owl was hollering in daylight when it was a night bird that carried the omen of death with it, a belief on the mountain that the owl screeched to tell of a person dying in the home nearest its call. Quickly, he tried to count homes closest to its call, and when he realized that there was open land between the call and his home, goosebumps broke out on him.

The wind came up early in the trees, and its sound was mournful enough. The sun was breaking through the treetops. And for ever so spare a moment Ishmael wished for rain, a reason for not planting corn. Yet he knew gauging the sky that there would be no rain this day. His ears picked up different sounds from those belonging to the mountain, and he stopped often to listen, sure now that somewhere among the brush and trees some of the boys who had heard his brag were trailing him. They followed out of curiosity and also to report back to others, set to build a brag of their own on how near the cabin they had trailed him. Any reports of his turning back would brand him a coward. He listened for give-a-way signs and hoped that the crows and blue jays would favor him and mark the trail of their following. But he heard only the wind, sightless and trembling the limbs on the trees like ghosts. He glanced with caution, not wanting those who followed to know that he was searching for them. He knew that they would hide sight and sound as carefully as if they were on a squirrel hunt.

He wondered how close to Hattie's cabin they would chance to follow, how strong their belief that Hattie was a witch. If they were remembering as he was that it cost nothing to believe but everything not to and be wrong. Unless he missed his guess, the older boys would be leading the pack, some his own age next, and the younger who had not already backed off bringing up the rear. He did not think any of them, including the oldest, would trail him all the way, believing their brag was stronger than their will. To tempt and be wrong in the least still carried a price too great to pay.

This side of her cabin he stopped to listen and to scout about with his eyes. And then, slowly, he edged on. He was close enough to smell the new turned earth before he reached the bottom. Given another time and reason he would have loved the smell. Reaching it, he stooped, and while he listened for sounds behind him sifted the black loam through his fingers. Worked by the harrow, the corn ground was smooth enough to hold bird tracks. More ground had been turned than he had thought, and he knew it would take a long day's work to plant it all, if he lived long enough to do it. Once planted, the seed would sprout quickly in the rich, soft earth within three or four days at most. He stared up ahead and then behind. He thought of turning back. Forward was the way to a witch, backwards the way to a coward. But for some strange reason he remembered the words of his mother that truth was stronger than superstition. Leaving any portion of the bottom fallow and facing her seemed the worst of the lot.

Around a bend in the creek her cabin came into sight, and he could see that she was standing on the edge of the porch. He was sure she had been told of his coming and was watching for him. He wondered what boys if any were still following. He judged they had come as far as the edge of the plowed field and then hid-off in the underbrush and waited, listening for screams or wails that might come from someone caught by a witch, sounds to offer them a quick start back down the hollow.

He swallowed and walked toward the porch wondering if whatever he said less than the truth could be seen through. Judging that he would be too scared to talk anyway, he edged on until he reached the porch. And then Hattie broke the silence.

"I been waiting for you, Ishmael." She brushed her thin hair from her face, blown there by a breeze off the sides of the ridges. "My, how you've growed since I saw you last! Old enough now to do a man's work." She squinted toward the bottomland below them. He saw that most of the field could be seen except for the far end where a tip of it was lost to a bend in the creek. "From here the field looks a mite smaller than it is," she added. "But many's the time I remember my Henry talking how it had a way of growing in front of a gooseneck hoe." She cackled, and Ishmael could see that she had lost most of her teeth and that her jaws were sunken. She was breathing through her mouth, causing her jaws to move back and forth like the gills of a fish out of water.

He tried to keep his eyes from her. She was even more witch-like uglier than he had imagined. So old that even his mother did not know her age. She was winter-thin, wind-tanned, and overall mountain-leathered and unkempt. Her voice was shrill and piercing like he had heard a witch's voice would be. And when she pointed off toward the bottomland her bony fingers looked no bigger than bird claws and were gnarled and bony. Thin wisps of hair caught in the wind even though she had tied most of it in a bun on the back of her head.

The yellow cat lay on the edge of the porch staring at him with eyes as yellow as a winter hedge apple. It caught him looking, ruffled its fur, and spat at him. Hattie scolded it, and the big bobcat-cross stretched back out on the porch catching the meager rays of a sun filtering down the slope.

"Rowdy don't see many strangers," Hattie said. "Good mouser and snake catcher."

For a moment Ishmael's heart beat fast. What a brag! He was now probably the only boy on the mountain who knew the cat's real name, that it was not Lucifer at all. But he probably would not live long enough to build a brag about it.

Back-bowed, Hattie was no taller than he was. But it was her eyes that held him the most. They were black as coal, the skin crow-footed around them. They were sunk in but not mean looking. In fact, he thought, they looked no different than the eyes of the other older women on the mountain he had seen. But then, too, he thought, this could be the way of a witch, looking natural enough to show the opposite of the way it really was!

"Known your mother and pa all their life," she said. "Fine people, true to a fault. Knew your grandma and grandpa too on your ma's side." She stared off along the slopes. "But they were born before your time. Your grandpa was killed inside a coal mine over on Blacky leaving your grandma to pine her life away lonesome like me."

For a moment now Ishmael felt sorry for her but remembered that pity could coax like a spider.

"Tell you what," she said, "you run on to the corncrib and get a double handful of ear corn to shell for seed, and I'll go inside and fetch you a brew to take the dryness from your mouth caused from your walk up the hollow."

She turned and Ishmael swallowed. He would have sworn he could see the big cat watching him closer now like it was expecting him to run once Hattie was inside the cabin. Standing now, he looked too big to be just one cat, even a cross!

Afraid not to follow Hattie's orders, knowing he could not outrun the cat, Ishmael turned toward the small crib built on the side of the ridge. He thought of his reward for getting the corn: a cup of henbane. The same brew that was said to have put Henry in his grave! He thought of a way out but nothing came. Drink the brew and his brag would be paid for; refuse to drink it and reap the same reward: shriveling up somewhere along the mountain for buzzards to find.

He opened the crib door and got a double handful of eight-row corn, enough that she had judged would be needed to plant the field. On the way back to the porch a thought came to him: whatever was in the brew with henbane, snakes, and the like would probably work slowly because she would need him to plant the corn first. But the thought offered no consolation.

Strange that while they sat on the porch shelling the seed corn, again she almost seemed ordinary. Except for the big cat seeming to begrudge the attention she was paying him and spitting at him now and then, he was spellbound by her talk and judged she might be the smartest person about things on the mountain he had ever listened to, including his own mother. She talked out of loneliness, a loneliness that only someone on the mountain could. A loneliness that he had known and still did during the long summer days. And—hoped he might again. In darkness a candle was better than no light at all.

When the corn was shelled and he had drunk the brew, assured that it was made from the roots of a red sassafras—and tasted like it—she reached over and patted him on top the head.

"My," she said, "you'll never know what company you've been to an old woman what's pining her last years away." She pointed again toward the cornfield. "Remember, there is enough corn seed to plant the field if you lay your rows straight. Your first row will guide the others. Just be sure all the rows are planted. For the rows of corn will be like the strings of a dulcimer later when the corn is tall enough to catch the wind. And it is the music of the corn that I am after. Windsongs that me and Henry used to always sit on the porch and listen to of the evenings when the wind came up. The wind plucking the rows of corn like strings and me and Henry catching the music." She brushed the hair again from her thin face. "I know it's foolish to want to listen to a windsong and pretend that Henry is sitting here with me, especially to a boy. Henry over there sleeping, waiting below troublesome grass. But I got to hold on to something." She rocked back and forth now. "Plant careful.

A missed hill will be like a song with a chord missing. My eyes ain't what they used to be, but my ears are still as keen as a squirrel's. Missed notes are easy to catch. But I got no worry about that with you. I knew you were special when you come. Enough like your ma and pa, truthful to a fault! Sent to pacify an old woman what's outlived her time on the mountain but can't choose the time of going. Lord does that."

She scolded the big cat again for spitting and then looked at Ishmael. "The music in the corn is all I got to look forward to this side of a winter that could be my last. Plant me a windsong, Ishmael."

She stepped inside the cabin and returned with a sack to carry the seed corn and a gooseneck hoe for planting. She handed him the sack but kept the hoe long enough to rub the handle. As if she might be thinking he saw it strange for her to keep a hoe in the cabin instead of the corn shed, she added, "I've always kept the hoe in the dry. It was Henry's favorite tool. Still carries his hand-marks."

She shooed Ishmael toward the corn bottom with a grin more scary than friendly because of the thinness of her face, a grin that could fit witch or friend!

Ishmael watched her now as she stared off toward the bottom, and as he walked off carrying the sack of seed under one arm and the gooseneck hoe over his shoulder, he wondered how far her eyes could follow and still pick him out. If what she said about not having the sight she once had was true or another way to catch him up, witch-like. He took her at her word on hearing since that seemed to be the less threatening of the two. If he lived he could be far away before she heard the cornsong.

As he walked he could feel the curve in the handle of the hoe, part whittle-made and part hand-made. Where the hands had fit— Henry's hands. He swallowed.

Once he reached the bottom his thoughts returned to the boys he felt sure had followed him. He wondered how many had waited him out and were watching now from where they judged to be a safe distance. He could feel they were there. Like the feeling of knowing that a squirrel was in a tree or a covey of birds in honeysuckle, the squirrel sure to cross out, the quail sure to flush out on you. Instinct that brought excitement and came natural with being a part of the mountain.

He thought of his brag: he would plant part of the field but trick the witch by leaving part of the cornfield fallow. He thought of the windsong she spoke of. And the windsong for some strange reason was what he had to weigh between a brag and the boys who were hid off. In the back of his mind he worried about depriving Hattie of her windsong and lying about it to his mother, who was sure to ask about his planting the corn. The choice was the possibility of being snuffed out by a witch, owning a brag bigger than the mountain itself, or being branded a coward for the rest of his life.

He thought of his chances of getting away with planting most of the field but leaving a row or two that faced the creek unplanted, being farther away from her sight. If her eyes were too poor to see, skipping the rows would buy him time, the time it would take for the corn to sprout and grow tall enough to catch wind enough to make strings like a dulcimer. And when that time came there was always the chance that the missed rows could be blamed off on muskrats that often pulled young shoots up by the roots, dragging them to the creek and into the mouth of their dens below the surface of the creek. If not muskrats, then crows!

The more he planted the more he thought of his brag. Unkept it would make him the laughing stock of every boy on the mountain and the end of every joke down at school. He could see them now gathered in the schoolyard pointing his way, whispering, making fun, and marking him a coward forever.

He thought of Hattie. Her life was short, and if she did not hear a song she wouldn't have to suffer long, but for him at his age time seemed eternal. It could be his mother would ask only if he had planted corn—nothing to indicate all of it. A nod could be taken more ways than one. Could be a lie could be hidden.

But thoughts of Hattie Milton still would not leave his mind. He saw the old woman sitting on the porch with only a crossed-up cat and a crippled muley cow for company. He thought of how ordinary she looked, nothing like he had expected. If asked what he had expected, he could not have answered. But surely not an old woman normal as a summer day, friendly to a fault. He saw visions of her sitting alone by the grave mound amidst the witchgrass, rocking back and forth, mumbling words in an unknown tongue, unknown to the mountain but understood by Henry, the only one the words were meant to be understood by. How for her loneliness was forever, happiness a simple windsong made by a mixture of corn and wind.

Planting the corn now he wrestled with what to do. One thing he did know: never again would he be a part of a hold-to-brag so hard to shed.

Continuing to work the field he scooped out pockets of earth and dropped in the seed. The world around him was silent enough to listen for sounds of the boys he felt sure were close enough to see him. Hoping without their knowing that he suspected their being there, he stole quick glances and caught what sounds he could while he wiped the sweat from his face and leaned on the hoe handle for rest. He could hear the low hum of the creek water over rocks in the bed and stared at the bobbing killdeers searching for food there. Catching movements in the brush, he waited to see if birds flew out to account for the movement or if some boy with nerve enough had sneaked closer. He was more sure they were there but could not see them. He knew they were mountain-smart and would be hard to catch. His whole world had turned into a not-knowing what to do. The sack of corn seed grew lighter. Soon he would have to decide.

The day grew long, the sun hotter, more than it should have for the month of May. But then, nothing seemed right this day. He thought of how right Hattie had been about the field growing bigger and bigger in front of the gooseneck hoe, a lesson Henry had taken to the grave with him. Scared, he swallowed, wondering if he might also take it to the grave before the day was done. The harder he worked the longer the field became, the broader it stretched. He stared off toward the cabin, but he could not see Hattie, only the frame of the cabin lost now in sun shadows. He doubted that she would be able to make anything out at this distance—he hoped. He stopped again when he neared the far end of the field to listen for telltale noises or signs of boys. But the birds were up singing now, not helping matters any. If boys were there he knew they would have chosen this end of the field. It was the farthest from the cabin and being so the safest. He doubted that any of them would strike Hattie's witchery off completely; the price of a risk was too high.

By the lightness of the seed sack he knew that his decision had to come soon. He was certain that the sack still held enough seed for two rows, the last rows facing up to the creek, rows that a muskrat would steal from if a muskrat was needed.

Nearing the far end of the field, Ishmael set his eyes on an old maple stump on the banks of the creek. Its top had been knocked off long ago by storm-lightning or washout. Staring at it, Ishmael made his decision. Sure that the boys were there he decided to gamble: give Hattie part of her song and keep all of his brag. A brag over truth.

He broke off a willow branch to wipe his tracks away and walked slowly but cocky-like up to the maple stump. It was even better than he thought for his purpose, short enough to reach without a stretch and filled in the top by dirt carried there by high water. Scooping out a pocket on top of the stump, he lifted out the seed that was left and, holding it high enough to be seen by the boys, dribbled the corn into the pocket, kernel by kernel, filling his brag to the very rim while they watched him cheat the witch. After the last seed had fallen from his hand, he pulled the dirt back over the seed and patted it smooth so that no one would be able to tell that the top of the stump had ever been touched. And now, walking backwards, he smoothed his tracks with the willow branch to wipe out signs that he had stopped there. Finished, he made his way slowly back toward the cabin knowing that going closer to the witch the boys would drop off one by one, gauged by their belief.

Hattie Milton was waiting for Ishmael. When he reached the yard she drew up a jug of tea that she had been chilling in the well. It tasted sassafras, the same as he had had before. But this time feeling more freedom since the first cup had not snuffed him out, he looked at the pure amber color of the liquid. It held no visible signs of the remains of snakes, toads, or chicken fat in it. Truth was, it tasted no different than the sassafras tea his mother made.

Hattie took the gooseneck hoe back into the cabin, cleaning the blade with an apron she was wearing even though Ishmael had washed it off in the creek to ward off rust.

She came back outside and smiled at Ishmael. "Took time to wipe the hoe blade down in bacon rind. Keeps the rust away, you know."

Ishmael sat with her until the night clouds showed above the ridges, listening to mountain talk, answering her questions about the world outside the head of the hollow. When he turned to go she took him by surprise, bent over and kissed him on the cheek. Her lips were cold and rough. Kissed by a witch!

"Lord bless you for planting me a windsong," she said. "I'll send payment down by Lief Potter end of the month when my pension comes."

"Ma says not to charge," Ishmael answered.

"And you?" she asked.

"Me neither," he said.

"Make no living by working for nothing," she said.

"I know," Ishmael answered, anxious now to get away.

"How you know something like that?" she said. "No bigger than a banty rooster." She grinned. "No matter. Reason for will turn you a favor one day." She bent over and almost in a whisper said, "Come listen to the windsong you planted for me when the corn grows tall enough."

Going home he wondered what it would have turned him if she knew that he had not planted all the corn. Worse yet, if she should find out. But he had chosen a brag over the truth, his wants over hers, and he set his mind to settle on that. Trying to pick up signs of the boys, he still saw nothing and heard only the birds quarreling close to roost time and the wind that swept out of the hollow now making little sounds on budding trees and new leaves.

Once home he was heaped with praise by his mother, who had spent part of the evening cooking his special meal. She was particularly pleased that he had not charged and spoke of rewards hereafter.

"Never know when will be the last crop for one so old," she said. "Other than with more loneliness than most, she has been time-blessed as it is."

It was well into a restless night that Ishmael realized the mistake he had made. His greed to keep a brag that should have never been made had caused a mistake he could not live with. He had lied to both Hattie and his mother. And soon both would know it. He thought of the praise from his mother, the special supper for honest work and her saying that truth was more powerful than superstition. He thought of Hattie, saw her turning her head, squinting toward a field of corn that was no more than a blur but listening for a windsong that would never be played. How old she was and maybe without enough time left to make another song.

In his haste to keep his brag, to show off to the boys who had followed, it dawned on him that his lie would sprout on him for the world to see! He wondered how he could have been so stupid as to plant the seed in the top of the stump without knowing full well that the seed would sprout into a lie. To be seen by Hattie if she ever made it down to the bottom. If not then, surely by Lief Potter or others who passed on their way up and down the hollow,

stopping to check on her before coming into Sourwood or crossing the ridge to their own home.

He worried into daylight and then moped around during the
day. So much so that his mother noticed and asked, "Didn't overdo
it, did you, Ishmael?"

Assuring her that he was fine, he loafed off in the garden and
then on to the side of the ridge cutting some poles for pole beans.
He searched for a way out. And toward evening, he knew there
was only one way. He would have to return to the stump and scoop
out and plant the last two rows of corn. He could not live with
telling a lie to his mother or to Hattie Milton. He had seen the
loneliness of the old woman, the sadness in her eyes, and then the
happiness with the thought of sitting another year on the porch
with her man long buried under the witchgrass listening to a song
as if it could lift him out of the cold ground like a rising fog in the
hollow after a spring rain. Ishmael had never intended his brag to
bring so much misery. There was little time left to make amends.
The seed would sprout soon in the rich earth.

He would plant the two rows after darkness, since the sky
spoke of a full moon to help him see. Also, he could use a weak
light from a miner's lamp. Knowing that it might take a while, he
decided to tell his mother he was going over to Richard Summers's,
who was wanting to try out a young bluetick on a night hunt.

"Wouldn't be working a young dog too much in green brush
with the weather turning hot," she said. "Female varmints are apt
to be in their ways now too and don't need to be bothered much."

"Richard don't mean to shoot out and keep," Ishmael said.
"Wants to see and hear what kind of nose and mouth the bluetick
is apt to grow up with."

His mother looked at the sky.

"Well, don't look like you'll be needing a whole lot of manmade
light with a full moon coming on. Be careful. I'll leave a lamp lit,
and if I'm asleep you can blow it out when you come in."

The moon was coming up early and Ishmael was glad. With

no reason for anyone figuring he would return to the cornfield, no one would be following. This made the going faster and easier. When he reached the cornfield, he thought how lucky he was for a full moon. Lucky until he came upon the stump. His hand felt the cupped-out earth in the top of the stump before he saw it with his eyes. The seed was gone! Knowing that a bird, even a crow, could not have dug it out that easily or have even sensed it was there as deep as he had planted it, he bent to search the ground around the stump for tracks. And he found his answer: footprints. Several of the boys had left their footprints around the stump with no caution at all. They had never expected Ishmael to return, to have reason to return. Their plan was a simple one: they would hold him to his brag if ever he should change his mind, a brag hard to top but that he could pay dearly for. He knew now that word would spread fast once the corn had sprouted that at least two rows had never been planted. Two unplanted rows were too many to blame on varmints, crows, or blackbirds. They would test to see just how brave he was, whether he believed Hattie Milton was a witch or not. Truth was, Ishmael still did not know. He wanted to believe she was just a lonesome old woman living alone like his mother had said. But tales of her spell castings, omens, and the sort had been ingrained in him since his first day at Sourwood School. And she had been blamed for too many things that had no other answers. And add-to he had wanted to believe. The excitement and mysterious things could be used on boys younger than himself.

This much he did know: the way things stood, if there was any truth whatsoever to her witchery he was past due to be snuffed out! Defying the witch would spread like wildfire on the mountain. Tales would sprout scary enough to raise the hair on your head, and he would be watched for changes that ought to come to a boy near the end of his days. No one would want to loaf off with him, figuring the witch would search him out and get them too. What a lonesome life his would be no matter how short!

There seemed no way out now. His tongue had dug his grave.

He stared off remembering the words of his mother, "I'm proud of you, Ishmael, proud that you planted Hattie a windsong! You will be rewarded by and by."

And then from nowhere a thought came to him. A thought that spread into a plan. He swallowed. Could he do it? Could he plant the corn? Seed—he knew where it was: inside the corncrib built to the side of the ridge at Hattie's cabin. If he was caught, he was a goner for sure; if he didn't try, he was a goner in more ways than one. The easiest way out was to try, to follow the path of truth. To believe as his mother had said that truth was stronger than superstition.

Ishmael turned up the hollow toward Hattie's, traveling high along the steep bluff. The going was hard and would get harder. The land was heavy with sawbriars that caught his ankles like snares, sawing his flesh and earning their name.

The closer he got to the cabin the harder the traveling. The land was new to him, ground that held too many tales for him to have traveled on and know. He did not know locations of the sandrocks and stobs, and both tripped him. The wind was up in the trees now, and a fire built in the potbelly to ward off the night chill belched grey smoke up the rock chimney, trailing off like ghost garments.

Seeing the corn shed below, he stooped to crawl but slid down the slope most of the way. What to do if he was caught was too scary to think about. He tried to temper his thought of being caught by seeing no reason why she should come back outside as late as it was. From her talk of Henry with him on the porch, he knew that she had already been to the grave, mumbled her words, and left him to witchgrass. He felt grateful for that.

Using the shadows of the shed to bank him from the moon, he slid down to the door. Glancing quickly toward the cabin, he lifted the latch.

He lost his breath! Sitting on top of the small doodle of eight-row corn was the yellow cat. Old Lucifer, big as a good-sized dog!

The hair on his back ruffled as if it had been combed to stand up. His eyes looked walnut-size, yellow and haunting as the eyes of a hawk. He sat motionless, as if he had known and was waiting for Ishmael's coming. Worse yet he could have been sent there by Hattie to wait him out. It seemed too much to ask of luck that he was there to keep mice out of the corn!

Too frightened to run, Ishmael stared at him. It was eyeball to eyeball now. No movement, no sound. Ishmael figured his luck had just run out. The big crossed-up cat would be his doom! Hattie had probably cast the spell and gone on to bed.

Ishmael waited for whatever was to come. There was no way he could outrun a crossed-up bobcat. He closed his eyes, swearing that no matter he would never brag again!

He stood for what seemed an eternity. And then he felt something rough and wet on his hand and heard the purr of a cat. Frightened and curious, he opened one eye and saw to his disbelief that the big cat was licking his hand. He heard its purr—too loud, he thought, with Hattie so close by. The cat rubbed his hand with its coarse face hair. And with Ishmael figuring he had just been given a new life as undeserving as he was, he reached with his other hand and patted the big cat, Rowdy to him but Lucifer to the other boys.

Time was short if clouds moved in, so he gathered some corn from the crib and headed back up the slope, quicker now to take advantage of moonlight.

The planting did not take long. Following the hills of planted corn was easier because the ground had not settled yet around the other hills. His rows were straight as the strings of a dulcimer. And all the time he planted he thought of his brag, of the boys who had stolen the corn from the stump to cast a shadow of doom on him and end his brag. He thought of how his world might change even more for the better once the corn sprouted—every row! For after the corn had time to sprout, the boys would sneak back to see and then spread word of the two unplanted rows of corn. How would they explain a bottom full of corn? Did a witch plant the rows? To believe that was to add more strength to his brag! A brag that he intended to let stand as it was. He had kept his word to them, kept his word to Hattie Milton, kept his word to his mother! He cleared his tracks by the stump so they would never know he had returned.

Reaching home late Ishmael heard his mother stirring.

"Young pup do all right?" she called from the other room.

"Fine," Ishmael answered.

"Good mouth on it?" she inquired.

"Deep and mellow," Ishmael said.

"Blow out the light before you lie down," she said.

"Yes'm," he answered.

Waiting for sleep he started work on his brag, mountain-size. A full field of corn would speak of witchery. But that was for the others to build on. They had held him to his brag, and he would hold them to their belief. In the meantime, he might just take Hattie up on listening to the windsong with her. Talk about a brag!

Love and a
Can of Worms

(An Appalachian Love Story)

On his way down the path to the cowshed Eli thought of how it had been that he had carried her books to school. He had been walking the mountain path to school with his older brother, Aaron, when Aaron had spotted Gunus and some of his friends up ahead and had hurried to catch up with them, leaving Eli to walk alone. Eli didn't mind. In fact he wanted to be alone. Without having to listen to Aaron, he could ponder how he was dreading these last days of school. He could meander alone and look toward the river where he knew the white perch were starting their run. He ought to be digging worms and heading to the river instead of being cooped up in school all day. But the thought of facing his ma for missing school kept him on the path. The white perch would have to wait until the weekend.

As he walked the path now he thought of worms. How hard they were to find and how his ma had said it was the hottest and driest May she could remember. The ground was so hard he could hardly dig in it. Worms were almost impossible to find. They had gone deep to find moisture. And so to coax them closer to the surface he had been carrying water to the cowshed for the past few days and soaking a spot of ground. He was hoping the worms would start moving up nearer the top of the land by the weekend. Nothing would catch a white perch like a redworm, and nothing at this moment meant more to him than catching white perch. He had dreamed of catching them over the long days of winter. He had imagined their drumming along the river, wondering how the music they made broke the surface of the river and spread over the land about. He had closed his eyes to see the cotton blooms cover the river willows—a sure indication that the white perch were running—and then fall soft as feathers to lace the water, whirling in long pearl strings along the bank. His world now was the world of the white perch, nothing else.

Walking the path to school and thinking of nothing else but white perch had caused him to stumble into her—that and a sharp crook in the path that had partially hidden her from sight. She had been carrying an armload of books, and he had caused her to drop them. She bent to pick them up, and without thinking, he stooped to help. That's when their eyes met. He had noticed that her eyes, soft and brown as buckeyes, showed no sign of being mad at him. She simply asked if he would help carry her books the rest of the way to school. And for some strange reason, without a moment's thought, he had wanted to. He had carried them as far as the big sycamore at the edge of the schoolyard before stopping to stare off, cautious. He was afraid that Aaron, Gunus, and some of the older boys, all bad to tease on something like that, would see him.

But he wanted to carry them farther. All the way to where she would sit inside the schoolhouse. He hadn't, but once inside he watched to see where she would sit and took a seat beside her, crowding out Ben Rice for it.

Listening to the teacher take roll, instead of thinking of white perch like always, he was thinking of how, when they had stopped to gather her books, their hands had touched. How her hands had felt as soft as the looks of a summer sun. There had been freckles on her hands but mostly on her nose, freckles that looked right and natural on her but wouldn't on anyone else.

He thought of how he had pulled his hand back, ashamed. For his hands were rough. Rough from grubbing on the mountain, hoeing the garden, forever cutting wood, and the sort.

He kept his ears keen to hear the teacher call her name. He found out that her name was Melissa Hewlett. Later that day he found out that she had just moved down from Louisa, a small river town farther up the valley. That her father had bought a lowland farm where the land was soft enough to poke a stick in for a hole to drop the seed into.

During the day he chanced a peek at her several times and swallowed when he caught her staring back with a smile on her face, mysterious enough to take his breath away. Whenever she answered the teacher it was with a voice as soft as a night wave along the river. And when school ended that day, instead of being happy that he was closer to fishing for white perch, he felt miserable. Hooked himself by something he couldn't understand and couldn't talk about without being teased off the mountain.

During the rest of the week, things got worse. Maybe it was his being so anxious to go to school that filled Aaron with suspicion, caused him to squint now, peculiar-like. Or maybe it was hanging off from Aaron, going alone to sit along the mountain where he could try to reason what had happened. What had stepped in and clouded his world of the white perch? Why did he feel both happy and mad? Happy that she favored him over Ben Rice, mad that she had come into his world so near the end of school and so close to the white perch run. As he stared off over the mountain, there was only one sure thing he was grateful for: the mountain would not tell his secret.

Near the end of the week, sitting alone on the mountain until the shadows had come, Eli made a decision. He would let nothing—not even Melissa—enter his world of the white perch run. His ways of the river and the mountain were stronger than anything else in the world, no matter how exciting and mysterious they were. He wanted nothing—absolutely nothing—more at this moment than a can of red worms. He would give up anything for them.

By the time he reached the cowshed early that Saturday morning, he had convinced himself that the world was as it was before she had come. That he cared only for worms and white perch. And so when he reached the shed and stopped to dig in the earth he heard once more the drum of the perch.

But digging in the hard earth he found that he was faced with yet another problem. Worms were going to be harder to come by than he had even imagined. Water that he had spread over the earth had done little coaxing. The hot sun had rendered the earth almost as dry as a Devil's Powder Puff. The dust rose and settled with the sweat on his face.

The sun was high and he still had less than a half can of worms, almost too small to thread on a hook. Never had he dug so hard for so few. Figuring that he had dug about all the worms he was apt to get and still have enough time along the river, he started to leave the cowshed and then stopped. He heard something off in the brush near him. Squinting from the sun, adjusting his eyes to the shadows, he saw Gunus standing nearby, thumbs hooked in his belt, and grinning.

"Aaron home?" he asked.

Noticing that Gunus was staring only at the can of worms now, Eli said, "Was when I left."

Gunus shuffled his feet in the dust and grinned harder. "What you got in the can?" he asked.

"Fishing worms. What else!" Eli answered.

"Thought so," Gunus said. "Time for the white perch to run. You figuring to go?"

Eli figured that Gunus had asked two questions that he had already known the answer to: that worms were inside the can and that he was going fishing. He also knew that the look in Gunus's eyes told that he was up to something that Eli knew would not be in his favor.

"What else would I dig worms for!" Eli said.

Gunus stared off toward a patch of horseweeds and then shuffled his feet again.

"Lots of reasons," Gunus said. "Like, digging worms is as good a way as any to take your mind off other things."

Eli swallowed. Wondered if Gunus had caught the secret he had shared only with the mountains.

"Like to have me a can of worms," Gunus said. "Hard to find, dry as it is."

Mad at both Gunus and himself, Eli said, "Want worms, dig worms!"

"Might not have to dig my own," Gunus said, a grin on his face.

Curious, Eli said, "How come?"

But Gunus never answered. He was staring off toward the patch of horseweeds again. Eli stared too, and then lost his breath. For there, knitted among the stalks and swaying in the slow wind like a white-laced curtain was a spider's web. Here and there a drop of morning dew was still on the web and the drops blinked in the sun like eyes. Near one corner of the web, half hidden by a horseweed stalk, Eli saw the black and yellow spider. Near the center of the web he saw the heavy zig-zag lines that the spider had made there . . . written there! Eli counted seven flies and one beetle in the web. He watched as the big spider scooted nearer the center of the web and stopped. Maybe watching and listening. Anxious. Willing to wait. A big black and yellow writing spider!

Eli tried to stare off, act as if it didn't matter. But it was hard to do on something like that. For Eli knew that it had been believed forever here in the mountains that the writing spider was an omen. Evil as a witch. And that if the spider heard and wrote your name across his web—like he had probably done to the seven flies and one beetle—you'd shrivel up and die before the sun went down. Gunus probably knew how Eli was on something like that: beliefs, superstitions, and omens of the mountain. Aaron had probably told Gunus that Eli was the worst of the lot! To make matters worse, Eli had once asked his ma about the writing spider. Her answer had been that not to believe was not worth the gamble. Eli remembered, too, how it had been that Aaron had hooked him for more than one favor, like cutting Aaron's share of wood, by threatening to give his name to the writing spider.

Eli felt miserable. Fighting superstitions and wondering if Gunus knew how superstitious he really was. Especially how much he believed in the power of the writing spider.

Gunus said, "Hate to give a name to a writing spider like that. Big one! But that's a powerful can of worms you got there and I'm itching to go fishing. Tell you what . . . you just loan me the worms and I'll pay back later."

Eli knew that Gunus would never pay back. He also knew that darkness would catch him trying to dig another can and he would have no time along the river. Eli stared off, thinking for a way out. But Gunus stripped him of time. For Gunus was clearing a spot of land in front of him now with his foot. And then, using his big toe like a pencil, he began to scratch letters in the earth: M . . . E . . . L . . . I . . . He stopped and grinned.

"Ain't your name I'm thinking about," he said.

Eli swallowed. Good gosh, he thought. Gunus knows! Knows for sure! He's aiming to give her name to the writing spider!

With the big world rendered down to only a name and a can of worms, Eli thought of all sorts of things. It could be that there was nothing to the legend of the writing spider. But if he was wrong, she could be snuffed out and their hands would never again touch for something strange to pass between them. The red clay of the graveyard would hide her forever. Snuffed out by a writing spider because Eli had taken a chance that what had been forever believed in the mountain country was not so. But, then, he had reasoned out that his world had returned to the mountain and the river. That fishing for white perch was all that mattered. He glanced at the spider, Gunus, the can of worms. Caught now by not one world but two: a world that he understood, a world that he didn't . . . and with time running out in both worlds.

Gunus said nothing, but his toe did. Slowly, the toe scratched over the patch of ground he had cleared, adding more letters: S . . . S . . .

Quickly, Eli stuck the stob he was digging with in front of Gunus's big toe, stopping it from scratching in the last letter in her name. He handed Gunus the can of worms and watched as Gunus walked off, laughing in the wind. Leaving him with a world he had chosen but did not understand.

Reliefing It

You take Deck Billips. Great big thing weighing over two hundred pounds, strong as a timber mule, hairy as a Hampshire hog, and ain't turned twenty-five yet. Worked on and off in the mines around Harlan, Hazard, Pike, and Elkhorn until one of them government people sidled up to him telling him how bad off he was but didn't have to be with what all he was entitled to, and the next thing you know he gives up working coal and moves into Sourwood where he's closer to the handouts. You think he'll associate with me? I mean, my watching him grow up and all, being like a daddy after his pa was killed in the mines up at Martin. I can pass him now on the road and say, "Howdy there, Deck. How you feeling today?"

And he'll hump over like a flogged rooster and say, "Not so peart this morning. Don't think I got enough thiamin today. Man needs about a hundred big ones a day to come out all right. If I get under, I'm down in my back!"

"A hundred big ones?" I ask.

"Percent, old man! Percent!" he answers.

Me, what do I know about percent or thiamin? I mean, I been on the mountain all day cutting and snaking logs. All I know

167

about what a body eats is what you can plant, grow, or grub off the land to eat, dry, or salt for keeping.

Deck, he never sees the sun come up. Lays off in bed most times until the sun is going the other way. Raises them big sapling arms to stretch and looks over at his wife, Ollie, who's beside him in bed and says, "What time is my relief appointment today!"

Ollie squints toward a fancy clock now instead of the sun for time and says, "Three o'clock. You got two hours yet. Can't you roll over and let a body rest! You know I'm low on riboflavin!"

Deck says, "Maybe so, but I can't go hurrying into a trip like this, my back being the way it is and all. It ain't no short distance from here to there. You'll need time to mix me a bowl of rolled wheat from that white box and drown it in dried milk like they say on the directions. Fixed right, I do believe it does a body some good. Careful and don't get it mixed with the hog middlings again. Look for the contract number on the wheat box. I can say it in my sleep: GR (P) 5719. Besides, the sack of middlings has the picture of a hog on the front of it."

Ollie yawns. "Think that will hold you all right?"

Deck says, "Being that I ain't today what I was yesterday and didn't know it, you might ought to mix some grits from that yellow sack of meal I got last week. Be sure that way. One hundred big ones of thiamin, 50 percent of that delicious riboflavin, 65 percent iron to grit my craw, and 80 percent niacin. It's a hard drive down there!"

Ollie stirs, complaining with her head.

"And try to get that riboflavin a little more done," Deck says. "I don't like it rare."

Why, the other day my woman, Lily, meets Ollie on the road and says, "My, but you're looking peart!"

And Ollie—big, strapping woman—says, "If'n you wasn't too old to see, you'd know better. I've got myself a headache as big as Sourwood Mountain! I told Deck I was low on thiamin. If I don't get 50 percent a day, it's a headache every time! And worrying don't help none. Poor Deck, down in his back again. He had to load his own grub last time. Them government people ain't got no sympathy. They'd force a corpse to work!"

Well, Lily fries me up an egg or two gathered from our own henhouse of the mornings before I go off on the mountain to work timber. Worrying and talking to my old mule, Maud, about it all the way to the timber and during work. Talking about things like what happens if the government decides to jerk the tit away. Wean 'em off. Knocks the sides from the trough! With them sucking now worse than a litter of pigs. Talking about stuff like riboflavin and the sort and then waking up one afternoon and finding the sow's gone, slipped the pen. They all start having headaches and back trouble, or thinking they have, which is just as worse. Low on iron! I mean, you think of that! Me, I've mostly just et what was there and never worried about what was in it. I come out all right.

I says to Maud, "It ain't like relief grub ain't been here before and that I ain't had my truck with it once. Been thinned down until I was akin to a blue racer snake. I still have pains in my joints I ain't sure but what come from it all. I'll tell you, them government people come down here in the thirties and put the quietus on us all. Started with grapefruits, mostly. And roads being what they was back then, most was shipped upriver by paddlewheel and turned loose on us."

The grapefruits come in all sizes. Little ones, big ones, and in-betweens. Ripe, rotten, and some green enough to gall like a green persimmon. They stored them in a little shed they claimed was in the center of town, stacked them up in little doodles like heard-say they did with cannon balls during the Civil War. Like the cannon balls what are still in the courtyard here in Sourwood.

We started right off fighting. Nobody could agree that they had built the shed in the center of town. People from upper Sourwood claimed the doodles favored the people in lower Sourwood, and the people in lower Sourwood claimed they favored the ones in upper Sourwood. And the middle got the better of the two. All agreed the shed favored the river rats.

There was skirmishes everywhere as long as our strengths held out. Brother against brother. The Civil War all over again.

"And how would you like your grapefruits fixed this morning, Effie?"

"Fry the insides and save the hulls for souping."

We did. I mean, tried to fix 'em every which way from here to slanchwise. But I'll tell you something I learned about that little grapefruit. Fix it any way you want and it'll come out the same: grapefruit! Tell you something else about it, too: you got no way of knowing how one of them little yellow or greenish balls can hone a man's nerves until you've been on 'em three times a day yourself. In less than two months, I could have split a weasel's hair with the littlest nerve in my body; set to box the ears off a man, woman or child without knowing why. I mean, that was the thing! The only thing we knew was that it was coming free. We never stopped to think that we had been getting along all right before being told we wasn't. About middle ways the hog. But being told we was in a bad way crept in and grew and spread like crabgrass. But it didn't have to be. Entitled to better. We forgot about seeds. Working was out and grapefruits was in. Thinned now and weak as bluejohn milk but nursing free!

There was no appointment back then. It was first come, first served. And the line at the relief shed formed early. Me and my brother Eb was always up and around the mountain before sunup and still fell in no closer to the shed than a quarter mile away. You could have camped the night up there and been no closer. Big, burly men up ahead of you, rowdy and staring, hoping you would try to buck the line to give them something to do while waiting their turn. Sacks under their arms and staring up ahead trying to see the shed and hoping there was something there besides grape-fruits. For rumors was spreading that beans and cheese was being added to the list of relief grub.

But grapefruits was all we saw. Everyone grumbled. The big looked for little ones to fight, and the little ones looked for places to run.

"Ain't no strength to grapefruits!"

"They put the runs to you until you're as thin as a winter calf!"

And then, just when the world around seemed like nothing more than a grapefruit, it happened! Beans and cheese was added to the list. And yet in all the trips me and Eb made now we never got a bean. Not enough to go around. It was first come, first served. The line was as dangerous as a rattlesnake.

"What a combination if you make it: grapefruits to loosen, cheese to bind, and beans to clean the barrel!"

Even looking like you wanted to buck the line could cost you teeth to eat with. Not so much because of the cheese but the beans. It was that way with me, too. I thought of beans now all during the day and dreamed of them at night. A bowl of beans to wallow spoonful at a time on my tongue until the hulls come off on their own and I let them drop one at a time to my belly.

Near the end of it all, a common white navy bean turned me into little more than a thief. I mean, I laid me a plan. I'd get me some beans at any cost. I thought about the long line of people and looked for weak spots. I finally found one. Rowdy as it was, there was one thread of decency left: respect for the elderly. Men with flowing white hair, back-bowed by time, wrinkled as a turtle's hide, were often allowed to move to the head of the line. Mostly sunken-jawed and scrapping along with little strength left. Hardly enough to hold out. I guess most figuring by their looks that they could be going for their last meal, eyes sunk in the head like dying candles.

"Eb," I said one evening, "what would you give for a bowl of navy beans?"

Eb, thinned out on grapefruits but with eyes now lit up like a miner's lamp, said, "Maybe my life if I could eat the bowl of beans first!"

And so, early the next morning before we left the house, I took my pocketknife and cut the hair from the back of his head. I pasted it to my face, talcumed it white, and when we headed for the relief shed I could have passed for a hundred. I practiced curving my back like a hunter's horn around the mountain and tucked a sack under my arms ready for the relief line.

It worked! It was like a dealer working an ace through a poker hand at the DEW DROP INN. I slipped a couple of times on purpose to fake weakness and rubbed pokeberries on my face like blood from a fall.

"Eh, God, get this old-timer to the head of the line before we've got a burial on our hands!"

And I might have made it if greed had not set in. Sensing that I was near the shed, I raised to see. To see the beans! But I raised too high. I mean, the wind caught me head-on and shaved me like a straight razor, blowing the white talcum away like smoke. It was like throwing a chunk of meat to starving hounds! They gouged and mauled me, and someone bit off enough of one of my ears to season a pot of beans if you had had some. They rolled me over the riverbank and left me for dead.

After dark, Eb come out of the bushes and helped me home.

Ma fussed and rubbed me down with poke-root juice, which burned my bruises like fire. And that evening while eating grapefruits, I squinted at poor Eb's head, bald as a cucumber in back and shining under the light of the oil lamp.

After that, no one trusted anyone! They'd reach out and grab some poor man and have him half dry-picked before they found out his beard was real. Brother against brother, weak against the weaker, all thinned out by grapefruits!

"Ma," I said one day, "if it ain't too late and if I ain't too thinned out and beat down, I'm giving up on relief and finding me a job!"

I looked and found. Saved enough to buy me a mule and went off to cut and snake timber off this mountain. Got myself hitched later, and me and Lily raised seven children.

"Deck," I says just the other day, "get off them handouts before it's too late. Don't dig your own grave."

"Shut up, old man!" he says. "I'm rowdier than a bear with this niacin under my belt and just might be looking for someone to skin out, old and crippled or whichever!"

Well, I worry about it. Every day. Up and down the mountain. All they got to do is push seeds in the ground. But they might never this time.